"For kids v ....
stories...with fast action, lovable characters
and an exciting plot."
MyShelf.Com

a DOG CaLLeD LeKa

2007 Eric Hoffer Award Winner
Young Adult Notable Book

2007 American Society For
The Prevention Of Cruelty To Animals
Children's Book Award Finalist

2007 Book Of The Year Finalist
ForeWord Magazine

Highlighted Title Award
Independent Publisher

Publisher's Weekly Magazine
2007 Cover Feature

2007 Featured Book Of The Month
AllBooks Review

a DOG called Leka

Willard Manus

Viveca Smith Publishing
McKinney, Texas

vsp

ISBN 978-0-9740551-3-8

Library of Congress Control Number
2006921581

Cover design by Audrey Elizabeth Smith

VSP

To My Grandsons

David Manus Kennedy
and
Michael Will Kennedy

Chapter One

The dog was the third stray to have badgered Ben Edgeworth that day.

He wasn't much more than a pup, a German shepherd mix, Ben judged. Not that Ben was an expert where dogs were concerned. He liked them well enough and, as a child, once had an Airedale, only to lose her to a speeding car, a sad and shocking experience that left him wary of ever becoming attached to another animal again.

Ben shooed the pup away. The dog, used to rejection, didn't react. Ben looked at him and shook his head at the pathetic sight the pup presented, with his skinny legs, bony face and filthy tail. He was mostly black all over, with patches of contrasting tan fur, and he smelled bad.

The boatyard, which was owned by a man named Petros, was full of dogs like this one, scraggly, ill and underfed creatures that no one wanted. They could find refuge here because the yard was unfenced and crowded with boats.

They could find food, too, thanks to the scraps of garbage left behind by workers and sailors. Otherwise uncared for, the dogs prowled the oil-stained grounds all day long, looking not only for food and water, but also a kind word or even an occasional caress.

Ordinarily Ben would have befriended the dog in some small way, but today he just couldn't be bothered. He had too much work to do on the boat he and Lukas, a ship's carpenter, were building together. The boat was a twin-hulled sailboat called a catamaran. Compared to other sailboats, a catamaran was a simple thing, a kind of glorified raft on pontoons, with two masts and space below deck for sleeping and eating. "Cats" were easy to handle at sea and relatively inexpensive to build.

Ben and Lukas had been working together on the boat for the past five months. They had started work on the day after Ben had received the insurance money coming to him from an accident which had taken his parents' lives. His parents were hired to sail a rich man's yacht from Gibraltar to a Caribbean island, where the man had just bought a home.

Ben had wanted to accompany his parents on the three-month journey, but because he was due soon to finish high school, they felt it would be better if he stayed put and concentrated on his studies.

"I know you'd rather be with us," his father had said, "but since you're so close to graduating, you might as well stick things out."

So Ben remained on Rhodes while his parents sailed off halfway around the world in a big, luxurious power boat. It wasn't the kind of boat his father and mother liked—they called them "bloats"—but they took the job because it paid well, providing enough money to enable them to start building their own sailboat when they returned to Greece. It had always been their dream to one day own a sleek, trim, twin-masted craft which would fly with the wind if handled right, making them feel happy and free. They would live on the boat and charter it out in summer, sailing from one end of the Aegean Sea to the other with four or five paying guests on board, combining business with pleasure.

For years they had been saving money to build their own sailboat, money they earned by minding and crewing other people's boats. It was a long, slow haul, though. The dollars you earned as employees didn't go that far, not when you were living outside the United States and had to pay private school fees to educate your only child.

That's why Ben was eager to be finished with school. It would help free his parents from their financial burden and allow them to start working on their own boat. Ben's parents had given up a whole other way of life when they first traded the USA for Greece. They had been high school teachers, but their abiding love of the sea had prompted them to resign their jobs. They went to work for a German industrialist who had advertised in a sailing magazine for a family to look after a yacht he owned, the *Kormoran.*

The German kept his yacht on the Greek island of Rhodes, which was located in the eastern corner of the Aegean, not far from the Turkish coast. Since working for the German meant being able to sail the fabled Greek islands in summer, Ben's parents decided to accept his offer. They gave up their apartment on Long Island, sold their car and most of their possessions, and moved to Rhodes. Ben was ten at the time. It was hard for him to break away from his friends and schoolmates and move to another part of the world, one which did not speak English as a first language. But over the years, he had come to love Greece. Living on the *Kormoran* and cruising on it in summer was a wonderful experience. He found it easy to learn Greek and make friends. Life was good, really—he counted himself happy and content—until the accident happened.

His parents were extremely skilled sailors who knew the sea well, having sailed up and down America's East Coast all their lives, but even they could not handle the freak storm that blew up as they were en route to Bermuda. It wasn't the hurricane season, but a hurricane struck nonetheless, almost without warning. They had tried to escape it by changing course and racing at full speed toward the nearest sheltering island, but the storm was too powerful, too savage and tricky. Forty-foot waves and sixty-knot, rain-filled winds had done them in. The boat capsized and eventually

4

sank, taking Ben's parents down with it.

"You must come home now," said Ben's Uncle James at the memorial service for his parents. "You are too young to stay on in Greece by yourself. You should come back and apply to college and get yourself some more education."

But Ben would not bend to his uncle's wishes. With the money coming to him, he could now do what his parents had only dreamed of doing—construct a boat of his own. Not just start on it, either, and build it little by little over the years. He could afford to put it together all at once. Not anything fancy like the forty-foot sloop his parents had dreamed about. It would have to be a much smaller, simpler vessel, like a catamaran. But, it would need to be seaworthy and roomy enough to live on and charter out to hardy sailors.

"That's an even more ridiculous idea," his uncle said, his voice rising with anger and disapproval. "Where do you get off thinking you could run such a boat as a business?"

"I'm a good sailor," Ben pointed out. "I learned from my parents and helped them on many a charter over the years. And I know the Greek islands well."

"I won't hear of it!" his uncle barked. "I won't allow you to toss your money away on some foolish idea!"

But Ben had just turned eighteen and was, in the eyes of the law, an adult. He could do what he wanted with the insurance money. Neither his Uncle James nor anyone else could stop him. Still, he knew he was taking a big chance with his life. He was completely on his own now and not too wise in the ways of the world. Sometimes, when he thought about the future, it seemed scary and threatening.

He owed it to his parents to be brave, to finish the catamaran and sail it around Greece, the way they would have done if they were alive. That's what they had wanted out of life, to be captains of their own boat, masters of their own fate. They hadn't been able to achieve that dream, but he could achieve it for them.

Finishing the catamaran was the only thing that mattered to him now. It took precedence over everything else, which is why Ben shooed the dog away by saying "Fige" to it, Greek for "Go away."

Lukas, who was standing nearby sawing a piece of wood in half, smiled and said, "How do you know he understands Greek? Maybe he belongs to one of the foreign boats in the yard."

"He doesn't belong to any kind of boat," Ben said. "He's too dirty and scared to be a seagoing dog."

Lukas, a tall, stocky, white-haired man with an equally white, curved moustache, put down his saw and studied the dog intently. "You're right about that," he said finally, "He's a scrawny thing, but there's something special about him. Just look at those eyes."

Sure enough, in those soft, brown eyes was something more than just the usual fear and desperation shown by the local strays. There

6

was an intelligence and sensitivity as unmistakable as it was unexpected. The dog's erect, wide-set ears added to the impression of alertness. Ben climbed the catamaran's ladder and went below to the galley where he had stored a few provisions. He searched among the cartons and cans for something that might make a meal for the pup, settling finally on a can of macaroni.

The dog smelled the food even before Ben came down off the ladder, whipping his tail from side to side with near-delirious anticipation. But when Ben put the can down and stepped back to watch the dog attack it, he was surprised to see hesitation on the mutt's part. He approached the food, all right, and put his face down toward it, but he would—or could—not eat, making whimpering noises in his throat instead.

"Maybe he hates macaroni," Ben joked.

The old man kept studying the dog. "He wants to eat," he said, "but he can't. Something is wrong with his digestion, worms, maybe."

"What should we do?"

The old man thought about it for awhile. Then he made up his mind:

"Give him olive oil."

"Olive oil?" Ben started to laugh. "Olive oil is for salads."

The old man's face darkened. "You know nothing," he spat contemptuously. "Olive oil is like a medicine. It's good for a hundred different things. You can put it on skin that's been burned by the sun, or rub it in your scalp to

7

prevent baldness. But it's especially good for
ailments of the stomach."

As proof, Lukas crossed to the shed where
he kept his personal belongings, returning
with a bottle filled with a thick, dark-yellow
liquid. "From my own trees," he said proudly.
"A first pressing, pure and rich as gold."

Lukas poured half the bottle of oil into a
plate and set it down before the dog, who
sniffed at it tentatively. It was an unfamiliar
smell to him. He looked up questioningly at
Lukas, who reassured him with a nod and
urged him in Greek, "Try it, it's good for you."

The dog took a lick. The taste went down
easily, and he looked up at Lukas again, this
time gratefully and trustingly. Returning his
attention to the plate, he began to lap up its
contents, not stopping until the plate was empty. Then he turned and, licking his chops, trotted off.

"We'll never see him again," Ben said.

"You're wrong," Lukas replied. "He's just
cleaning himself out."

They resumed work on the catamaran,
which, after all these months of hard labor,
was nearing completion. So absorbed were they
in their chores that they hardly noticed the
dog's return an hour or so later. This time the
stray went right to the macaroni and began to
wolf it down. It was almost comic, the speedy
way he ate, jaws chomping away non-stop, con-
centrating so hard that Ben and Lukas were
completely forgotten. In a matter of minutes,
the dog devoured his meal in huge, noisy gulps

punctuated by the excited whacking of his tail.

He kept going too, licking away at the insides of the can, cleaning it so thoroughly and brightly that it shone like burnished silver in the morning sunlight.

It was only then that the dog looked up, with such gratitude and love that Ben, against his will, felt his heart go out to him.

Chapter Two

The dog never left Ben's side after that, just sat in the shade, panting, watching everything the boy did with his keen, bright eyes. His patience and loyalty were matched only by his intelligence, which he showed when Lukas, standing on the ship's ladder, dropped a chisel he'd been wielding with his powerful but gnarled hands.

Lukas let out a Greek curse only to have it turn into a cry of admiration when he saw the dog cross to where the chisel had fallen. The dog not only picked it up, but carried it in his jaws to the foot of the ladder, where he waited for Lukas to come down and claim it.

"This dog is a marvel!" Lukas exclaimed. "You've got to keep him," he added, "I've never seen another mutt quite like this one."

While Ben tended to agree, he couldn't bring himself to declare allegiance to the dog. He knew from others just how difficult it was to care for a dog at sea. On top of that, the catamaran he was building was a small one, just twenty-four feet long, which meant space would be tight. The dog would be in his face every minute of the day.

It would also be an extra expense to maintain a dog. Ben had to be careful about money, if only because the catamaran was proving more expensive to build than he had estimated. Lukas was a skilled carpenter, but he was old and worked slowly, making for extra paydays. Also, Ben found that while most basic materials were available on Rhodes, things like spars, shrouds and sheets had to be imported from abroad with heavy duties attached.

Ben had enough money to finish the cat and get it launched. But he'd have to do without a ship-to-shore radio and other electronic equipment, maybe even an outboard engine. He would also have very little pocket money to cover daily expenses such as port fees and provisions. Keeping a dog might break the bank.

Fortunately, he had a charter lined up. The Smiths, an American family living in Paris, had answered his ad and were coming down to Greece in September to rent the boat, with Ben as captain. Ben would meet them in Athens. They were due to send him a deposit within the next few weeks, a sum sizable enough to sustain him in the months to come. If he could only find another couple of charters, his financial problems would be solved.

Since there was nothing the old man could do about them, Ben hadn't discussed these problems with Lukas. Lukas had worked all his life in Petros' yard, beginning as a ten year old apprenticed to his father. Lukas cared about building boats, not the sailing of them. He had come to work every day for sixty years, carrying his tools in an old, paint-stained box— tools that had been in his family for generations—and putting in his eight hours without complaint, shaping and assembling wood like a magician. Ben could never have built the cat without him, but he wouldn't dream of bothering the old man with his troubles.

Lukas communicated with Ben in a mixture of English, Greek and Italian. The latter he had learned as a boy, having grown up on Rhodes between the two World Wars, when the island was an Italian colony. He'd learned Italian in school and on the job, along with a smattering of other languages picked up while working for some of the foreigners who had dropped anchor at Petros' boatyard over the years.

Ben had learned much from this master craftsman with the flowering moustache and sun-baked skin. Ben's debt of gratitude was matched only by his admiration for the old man. He respected everything Lukas said and did, and almost always followed his advice— except when it came to the dog.

It just didn't make sense to become attached to this mutt, smart and likable as he was. Soon the cat would be finished and he would set off to sail the Greek islands. Even if he could afford to keep the dog, having him aboard would only cause problems—problems of sanitation, safety and practicality.

He mustn't forget the Smiths, either. Suppose they didn't like dogs or were afraid of them? It could make for trouble.

Ben made up his mind to part company with the dog before he became too attached. Abandoning him was out of the question, though. Ben's heart wasn't that hard. The least he could do for the pup was to find him some kind of home. But where and with whom?

Lukas was no help. As he explained, the notion of having a pet was foreign to most Greeks. There were a lot of cats in Greece and while people fed them, they rarely brought them into their homes. As for dogs, they were kept only as hunting companions and lived in pens outside the city. Most ordinary Greeks could not afford to maintain a dog.

Ben approached the other people in the yard, but even those who owned large and luxurious yachts turned him down. As one British skipper said, "Dogs and the sea are not compatible."

Lukas suggested just leaving the dog in the boatyard, where he would look after him as best he could and make sure he got fed at least once a day. But Ben didn't think much of the idea. The yard was filled with dangerous strays who were desperate for food. Chances are, they would tear apart a smaller, weaker dog in the war of survival being fought out daily here.

Lukas' next suggestion was the pound. He had never seen it himself, he admitted, but he'd heard that one did exist—a place where strays

13

were cared for in a safe environment and where the odd person who loved pets could come in search of an adoption.

Later, after making inquiries, Ben borrowed Lukas' motorbike and rode out to the nearby village of Koskinou. It took some doing to locate the pound, which was nothing like he had envisioned. In his mind, it was an American-style structure: a big building with offices, kennels and exercise yards.

Instead what he found was a barren field with a high wire fence around it. Under a tin-roofed shed about a dozen dogs lay listlessly in the shade. They were in such poor condition that they made the strays in Petros' yard look like the pampered dogs of the rich.

Unwashed, sick and underfed, the dogs were so weak that they could barely find the strength to raise themselves and inch over to him. Sickened, Ben turned away, but not before noting that there was no attendant or veterinarian on the premises. The place stank from the garbage serving as the dogs' fare and from the waste that stained the earth.

As he rode back to the city, Ben came to a conclusion—there was no way he could leave the dog behind. When he launched the catamaran and set off on his maiden voyage around the Aegean, the dog would be there.

Chapter Three

Lots more things needed to be done before the catamaran could be considered finished. Now that the mast and boom were up, the shrouds, sheets and halyards had to be installed, as well as four hundred square feet of sail. With the dog on his lap, Ben bicycled back and forth between the boatyard and the supply shops in Rhodes city, buying last-minute bits of equipment and provisions.

Through it all, Lukas kept working away, sawing wood and driving nails in a concentrated effort to finish off the carpentry work. The cat was a stubby little thing, it could have been twice as long, but so many things needed to be done. The dog was part of all the activity, never leaving Ben's side, not even when he crawled into a tight, dark space to tack up wiring or slap some paint around.

Lukas marveled at the way the dog not only stuck by Ben, but also helped him as best he could. After a few weeks, all Ben had to say was "hammer" or "pliers" for the dog to turn

15

and scamper off with his tail wagging, so happy he was able to be of help. "He must have been a very clever person in a past life," Lukas said. "I never believed in reincarnation before, but this dog has definitely changed my mind about it."

Lukas grew so fond of the dog that he helped Ben clean him up with baths and brushings. The old man even helped trim his nails and check his mouth for inflammation and odor.

"I'm no longer a carpenter," Lukas said with a grin. "I'm a dog doctor."

He kept urging Ben to give the dog a name—and, while he was at it, to name the catamaran as well. "It's time to pay both of these beauties the respect they deserve," he said.

Naming the boat was the easier of the two. As a boy back on Long Island, Ben had always liked to read about—and to sketch and paint—wild horses. He was also fascinated by the story of Crazy Horse, the warrior chief of the Sioux nation who had, against all odds, defeated the powerful army of General Custer at the battle of Little Big Horn. Putting those two interests together, Ben painted a swift-running wild horse on one of the cat's twin hulls, and a portrait of Crazy Horse in full-feathered battle dress on the other. Crazy Horse's name also went on the stern in big white letters.

As for the dog, well, that was a harder decision. Should he name him after a relative or friend? Making up a name was a possibility, perhaps something cute and funny, like Pinky or Boodles. That last thought made Ben wince. The dog deserved a more dignified name, even a European-sounding one. Something distinctive, like the dog himself. Lukas suggested a few Greek names, but they just didn't sit right—too complicated and too hard to pronounce. Ben wanted the dog to have a name anybody in the world could utter, easily and clearly.

Days went by, but no decision was made. Then came the morning on which a flock of strange-looking birds—they had round bodies and long slender necks—flew overhead. About a dozen of them were winging north in a V-formation so precise it looked as if it had been rehearsed. The birds flew swiftly and gracefully, working their long, curved wings with a minimum of effort, making rusty-door noises in their throats.

"What kind of birds are they?" Ben asked the man standing next to him, a Polish skipper named Zygmunt.

Zygmunt could not think of the word he wanted in English. So he repeated it in Polish several times. To Ben's ears it sounded like "Legga, legga."

When Zygmunt saw the confusion on Ben's face, he switched back to English. "This bird, she bring the babies."

"The babies?" Ben repeated, still befuddled.

"When they born. Deliver to mothers."

Ben comprehended, and laughed. "Storks, you mean. Storks."

Zygmunt nodded. "In Polish, leka."

Ben liked the name, for a lot of reasons.

17

Everybody loved storks, whether they really brought babies or not. They lived in groups, had families and stayed together. According to Zygmunt, who had been sailing around the Aegean for many years, the storks wintered in the hills of nearby Turkey and journeyed to the northern lake country of Greece when the weather turned warm.

They were definitely European birds, then, and had a distinctive name which rolled nicely off the tongue. "Leka" was close to the name of the first dog in space, Leika. It was also a little like Lukas' name, too. Leka and Lukas. Ben liked that. Every time he uttered the name it would remind him of Lukas, the man who not only helped him to build his catamaran but who also discovered the dog's finer qualities—and saved his life with that big dose of olive oil.

Lukas had been a father and teacher to Ben, educating him not only in the ways of building a boat but also in the ways of Greece and Greek people.

The old man with the blazing white moustache was flattered and delighted to be linked with the dog in this fashion. "I'm honored to give my name to this bright little fellow," he said. "As you know, my wife and I never had any children. I will always think of Leka as a kind of godchild, carrying on for me when I'm gone."

As a present, Lukas gave Ben the bottle of olive oil that had saved Leka's life. He also insisted on some kind of formal ceremony when the catamaran was finally launched. He paid for a Greek priest to come and bless the boat, and when the invocation was concluded, topped it off by pouring a glass of wine into the sea.

"This is what the ancient Greeks did," Lukas explained, "by way of paying homage to Poseidon, God of the seas."

It was more than just a ritual gesture on Lukas' part. Pleased as he was that Ben's boat was finished and seaworthy, he also felt a deep concern for the boy.

"You are only eighteen, a very young age to be captaining your own boat," he said. "It's not just your youth and inexperience that worries me—and the fact that you are sailing without benefit of radio or engine. It's the sea itself I fear."

The Aegean Sea was a capricious and dangerous thing, in Lukas' estimation. One minute it was calm and benign, the next stormy and angry. The Aegean had challenged seafaring folk from time immemorial with its sudden storms, nasty winds and awesome power.

"It looks beautiful and romantic much of the time, especially in summer, but it can turn on you without warning," Lukas said. "That's why I've always been content to build boats and not sail in them. Life in a boatyard may be repetitive and hard, but you don't risk death here, the way you do out on the waves."

Lukas begged Ben to be cautious when sailing, to resist taking chances. "Respect Mother Nature," he urged. "She is always more mighty than all of us poor souls put together."

Ben tried to reassure the old man. "I've sailed in all kinds of boats and weather," he reminded him. "I've learned navigation from my parents, and I know how tricky the Greek sea can be."

Ben also pointed out that a catamaran was a safe boat, easy to sail and handle. Because it had no keel or weight in the hull, it meant that in a bad storm he could pull into a cove and beach the boat if necessary. Besides, the *Crazy Horse* had been built by a true master, one who had seen to it himself that every nail was driven deep, every strut and spar placed perfectly. Ben promised Lukas that he would be a careful captain—particularly with a young dog on board.

Not that Leka was so small anymore. Thanks to healthy and regular food, he had put on nearly five pounds and grown several inches since joining them a month ago. Now to go with his bright, shining eyes he had a glistening coat and sturdy frame. His thighs were strong and muscular, his chest deep and full. So confident and healthy did Leka look that it came as a shock when he refused to take his place on the newly-launched *Crazy Horse*.

The transition from land to sea seemed to have upset the dog. He would not let Ben put him on the bridgedeck, wrenching out of his grasp and fleeing to the safety of the nearest slipped boat, where he slunk under the hull and hid himself, shivering and whining piteously. "Here, Leka," Ben called, softly, comfortingly. "Come on, boy, come back here." But the dog only shrank back further into the darkness and refused to budge.

Lukas once again mulled the problem over, concluding that Leka was afraid of the sea. "I'll bet he had a bad experience once," the old man ventured. "Someone must have tossed him into the drink and almost let him drown."

Great, Ben thought. The dog I'm sailing with is a nautical neurotic, he's allergic to seawater.

If it were any other dog but Leka, Ben would have abandoned him, if only because of the time it would take to help him overcome his fear. If indeed he would ever get over it.

But it wasn't any other dog, it was Leka, the dog he loved.

So slowly and patiently, Ben worked with Leka to help him get used to being at sea. He did it by first taking him for long walks along the shore, keeping a reassuring lead on him. Leka finally learned to frolic in the surf, then to enter the water up to the top of his hocks.

Eventually, by using ropes, one of which was tied to the *Crazy Horse*, the other to Petros' dock, Ben managed to coax Leka to begin swimming. Then he freed him from the harness, standing alongside him in shallow water to help and encourage him when he began to panic and founder.

It took a couple of weeks but finally Leka not only began to swim without fear, but actually began to like and enjoy the experience.

Pretty soon Ben couldn't get him to quit

paddling around. He had to pretend to be angry and shout at him, again and again, to get Leka to come ashore and shake the salt water off like a hoochy-coochy dancer.

Chapter Four

"Coming about!"

Ben uttered the words of warning as if his crew member were human, not canine, but Leka understood him nonetheless, scurrying from the starboard to the port side of *Crazy Horse* as the swirling wind suddenly changed direction and forced Ben to alter the mainsail.

Ben smiled at Leka, still tickled by the dog's innate intelligence. Not only did Leka understand his commands, he sometimes anticipated them, moving unbidden about the boat like a veteran sailor. He stayed close to Ben when the seas became rough, sometimes even went below when it was prudent to do so.

It could not be said, though, that Leka enjoyed sailing, not yet anyway. The fear he had shown as a pup in Petros' yard came out in harsh weather when the cat began to toss and pitch. If he weren't hiding in the galley, he would scrunch himself into a corner of the cockpit, with his ears tucked back, head down on his front paws, and tail tucked between his haunches.

Leka liked it best when they moved into the safety of a harbor. He would jump friskily and try to make himself useful. He even came up with a trick that startled Ben. It happened when they were still shaking down the *Crazy Horse* after it had been launched from Petros' yard. Every day for a week Ben took the catamaran out for short runs around Rhodes, to test the boat's sails and seaworthiness and build up his own confidence as a skipper.

Though he had acted cocky with Lukas, Ben knew that he still had much to learn about sailing. It was one thing to cruise in the company of your parents, another to venture out on your own. Also, he would be at the helm of a sailboat, not a power launch. He could not count on an engine to get him out of trouble. All responsibility rested on his shoulders. It was enough to give him many sleepless nights.

One of his nightmares came true a few days later, when they were returning to the Mandraki, Rhodes' main harbor. Ben had a difficult time trying to ease the *Crazy Horse* into its slip. Because he did not have an engine, maneuvering the cat in a small, tight area was tricky, especially for a lone sailor. Ben had to drop anchor and rush forward to toss a line ashore, all the while trying to avoid bumping into the moored boats on either side. He found himself dashing this way and that, doing three things at once.

Leka watched all this carefully, noting Ben's panic and anger. The next day, the dog was ready to take action when they entered the Mandraki and neared the dock. Seizing the line in his jaws, Leka leapt overboard and swam toward the shore, struggling to keep his nose above water. When he reached the dock, Leka dogpaddled in one spot, waiting for someone with a boathook to take the line and secure it to a bollard.

After that, it became a ritual that Ben and Leka repeated every time they docked the *Crazy Horse*. The Rhodians lined the shore when the *Crazy Horse* came close, just to catch sight of Leka in action. Ben would let go of the halyard, drop anchor and scoot forward to toss a line out. Leka would leap into the sea, clamp his teeth around the line and swim dockside with it, to the cheers of everyone watching.

"Bravo!" they would shout, "Bravo, Leka!"

When those onlookers went home, or visited a coffee house or taverna that night, they would talk about Leka's exploits. It didn't take long for the dog to become famous in Rhodes, and for children and adults alike to sing his praises.

Leka exhibited other startling traits during the first voyage of the *Crazy Horse*. One of Ben's biggest fears concerned Leka's toilet habits: what would happen when the dog had to relieve himself at sea? A cat could be trained to use a box, but a dog was another matter.

Once again, without being told, Leka seemed to understand what was required of him. He did not attempt to relieve himself while they were underway, waiting patiently until they reached the shore.

This could work only because of the unique nature of sailing in Greece. The Aegean was dotted with thousands of islands, many of which were, admittedly, little better than stone clumps rising out of the sea, like mushrooms. One could always see land, unlike the Pacific and Atlantic where one could sail for days and weeks without seeing anything but water and sky.

Thanks to this unique geographical feature and to the equally unique structure of the catamaran, with its shallow draft and light weight, Ben could easily beach the boat in just a few inches of water, allowing Leka to leap ashore, scamper off and do his business in natural fashion.

Leka saved his most spectacular trick for the third day of *Crazy Horse's* maiden voyage, when they touched down at a small nearby island called Alimos. They had enjoyed a long but splendid day of sailing. The prevailing wind on the west side of Rhodes—called in Greek the *meltemi*—had blown at a steady eight or nine knots, allowing the *Crazy Horse* to whiz along on its twin hulls. Ben had made a few mistakes at first, especially in the way he positioned the sails, but gradually he began to captain the cat with more confidence and skill. By the time they reached Alimos, he was not only handling the tiller and sails with ease, but staying firmly on course and getting maximum speed out of the meltemi. It made him feel a lot better about himself.

Just a handful of families lived on Alimos and even then for only part of the year. They were shepherds who kept flocks of sheep. Twice a year the animals would be rounded up to be milked and shorn of their dense coats of fur.

Just such a round-up was in progress when the *Crazy Horse* dropped anchor. Ben and Leka were invited by the hospitable islanders to watch the proceedings. The shepherds had gone into the hills some days earlier to find the scattered members of the flock, who were allowed to roam far and wide to find food for themselves—clumps of thyme and basil, low-lying branches of pine and olive trees, the succulent tendrils of crocus and cyclamen.

Some of the hardy, sure-footed sheep climbed to the tops of steep mountain peaks or ventured out on sheer-dropping cliffs to forage. It was a dangerous endeavor, but the sheep had no choice but to risk their lives. Alimos, like most Greek islands, was rocky and barren, having been denuded of its trees many years ago when protecting the environment was an unheard-of notion.

The shepherds had to be equally nimble themselves to negotiate the dangerous passes and trails, which were as familiar to them as each and every one of their sheep. The shepherds could tell one sheep from another even though to an outsider like Ben they all looked alike at first glance. But one had black fur around its ankles, another wore a cluster of small bells around its neck, another had spots here and there.

27

Slowly and methodically the shepherds, both male and female, young and old, had worked to gather the flock, guiding its bleating, protesting members to a central pen down on a dusty field not far from the waterfront.

The sheep didn't seem happy about being herded together and their thin voices kept rising in protest as they rubbed and bumped against each other. The shepherds had to shout to be heard over the din.

"Hummm!" they called, some from the backs of donkeys as they rode this way and that, trying to make the sheep obey. "Get back there!" they cried in Greek, "Keep moving, keep moving!"

The sheep kept resisting as time went on, giving angry cries and making other bleating noises. They kept trying to run for the hills every time the shepherds struggled to force them into the pen.

One section of the pen must have been weakened over the years because it suddenly gave way with a loud <u>crack</u>! In the next instant, sheep began spilling out of the break and scampering every which way. The shepherds began shouting and running after them, trying without success to shoo the animals back. It was chaos, pandemonium, a kind of madhouse.

Only Leka reacted decisively. Springing up, he chased after the sheep, barking furiously at them as he stopped their flight and turned them back toward the pen. Within a matter of minutes the frightened sheep were headed off and rounded up. They protested piteously but the determined Leka never faltered or erred in his work and soon restored order and obedience to the flock.

One of the shepherds, an elderly, stooped man in black baggy trousers and high leather boots, came over to Ben, a look of urgency on his face.

"Where did your dog learn this?" he asked.

"I don't know. He's only a stray."

"You mean to tell me you didn't buy him from a shepherd?"

Ben explained how he had found Leka in a boatyard and taken him in, though he did recognize that the dog had German shepherd blood in him.

The shepherd's expression turned incredulous. "The dog is one in a million," he exclaimed, adding, "I want him."

"What do you mean?"

"I mean exactly what I said." The shepherd was serious and intent. "I'm willing to buy the dog from you."

Ben looked over at Leka, who was sitting before the break in the fence, guarding it while he panted heavily, recovering from his frantic exertions in the sun.

"He's not for sale," Ben said. The shepherd took Ben's arm and led him to his small, jerrybuilt house. A table and chairs had been set up under a plane tree which cast a huge pool of comforting shade.

The shepherd's wife brought some glasses of water, a plate of fresh, rich cheese, a handful of black olives and chunks of brown, homemade bread.

"A dog like him is gold to us," the shepherd explained after they had broken bread together. "I can promise you that he will be treated accordingly. I know how badly some Greeks treat dogs, but this won't be the case with us. Leka will become part of our family."

The shepherd added that he expected to pay for the dog—and pay well.

"I'll give you seven hundred and fifty dollars for him," he said, after more discussion. "That's a small fortune for us, but I feel he's worth it. And he will undoubtedly sire other good dogs for us when he is older."

Sitting on the deck of the *Crazy Horse* that night, under a black but clear sky with a sprawl of stars blazing brightly overhead, Ben mulled over the shepherd's offer. The money involved was a tempting amount. After the unexpectedly high costs of building the catamaran, Ben was running low on funds. He had called the Smiths in Paris and left a message reminding them about the deposit, but they hadn't responded yet. He supposed that in a pinch he could always call his Uncle James and ask to borrow money, but that was a last resort. His uncle would surely make him promise to give up the catamaran and come home.

That would not do. No matter what, he would not give up trying to survive on his own here in Greece. He owed it to his parents to keep up the good fight, the way they would have if they were still alive. Selling Leka to the shepherds was a tempting way to solve all his financial problems—the money would give him a cushion he could ride until the Smiths paid the money they owed him.

Could he really sell Leka, though? He had fallen in love with the dog and would suffer greatly if he had to give him up.

On the other hand, he also had to take into account Leka's well-being. The dog seemed happy sailing with him on the *Crazy Horse*—but he had never shown such happiness as he did today, rounding up those sheep. The German shepherd part of him had come to the fore in a natural, spontaneous way. Leka had done what he was born to do—control and protect other animals. It had made him supremely happy and proud—the way an artist feels when he has painted a good picture.

Wouldn't Leka be better off being part of a shepherd's family than bouncing around the Aegean on the deck of a tiny boat? Ben glanced over at Leka. He was with the shepherds right now, curled up sleeping by the side of the children he had frolicked with all afternoon. The island had resounded with the children's excited laughter and the dog's equally joyous yelping. This was a good place for Leka, no doubt about it. He would have a home and a family and work he was born to do.

How could Ben keep him from all that? Wasn't it selfish of him to try to turn him into a sailor? In the end, Ben decided to leave things up to Leka. The dog was intelligent enough to know what was best for him.

31

So when the sun came up, Ben made ready to depart from Alimos, knowing the noise of the anchor chain being cranked up would rouse Leka and bring him to the shore. Minutes later Leka stood watching as Ben unfurled the mainsail in order to catch the wind.

Leka looked from him to the children who were standing behind him, watching things intently. Not far from them was the old shepherd himself, leaning on his walking stick. Leka glanced at him as well. Then he turned and looked out across the water at Ben.

Ben's gaze went to the shepherd. You can have Leka if he wants to stay, he thought. I don't want any money for him. How can I put a monetary value on such a dog, anyway?

Leka trotted down to the shoreline as the catamaran came about and slid out to sea. The dog seemed indecisive as he stood there, eyes darting back and forth between the children and Ben.

The breeze picked up a little and the *Crazy Horse* began to clear the quay which protected the small harbor. Leka trotted out to the end of the quay, the better to catch a glimpse of Ben and the *Crazy Horse*. The children followed behind, looking solemn. Ben, at the tiller, glanced back at Leka, who stood in rigid confusion, watching him go.

"Bye," Ben said, softly, sadly, "Bye, Leka."

The dog reacted suddenly, as if he had heard that whispered farewell. With a spring, he leapt into the water and started swimming frantically toward the *Crazy Horse*, his large black nose showing just above the waves and his brown eyes glittering anxiously in the sunlight.

Ben dropped the mainsheet, leaving the sail to flap around limply. The *Crazy Horse* slowed and stopped, bobbing about on the hard-blue sea.

Moments later Leka reached the *Crazy Horse* and was hauled aboard by its skipper. The two of them had a joyous reunion on the deck, with Leka barking furiously as he licked Ben's hand and shook seawater all over him.

Chapter Five

By the time the *Crazy Horse* reached the island of Symi, nearly a week had gone by. The winds were so weak that not even a catamaran could make much way. And since the *Crazy Horse* did not have an engine to supply auxiliary power, it was a long, slow journey. Often they were becalmed and still, left bobbing on the waves like a piece of flotsam for many long hours.

Ben used the time to complete various chores—and to get to know Leka better. The dog was slowly becoming less afraid of the waves, though he didn't like it when the boat keeled over in rough weather and righted itself with a loud smack. He never got seasick, though, but he did need to take two naps a day, one in mid-morning, the other toward late afternoon. His favorite place of rest was on a pile of curled-up rope under a patch of awning which gave shelter from the scorching Greek sun. It was his personal space.

Leka also liked to eat and drink right after

waking up, so Ben made sure to set out a dish of fresh water and a bowl of dog food at dawn. Immediately after that, Ben would head toward the nearest clump of rock or tiny island so that Leka could relieve himself.

After that, Leka would take his place by Ben's side, watching him as he worked the sails and tiller. Only when the sea blew up did he turn away and hide his eyes.

When they finally dropped anchor in Gialos, Symi's main port, Ben was amazed to see the hordes of people waiting on the quay for Leka to do his mooring-line trick. Obviously, the dog's fame had preceded his arrival.

"Ella, Leka," they called from the shore, "Leka, come on!"

Shouts and cheers followed Leka's successful delivery of the line. These island folk had seen a lot in their time, but never a dog that could swim ashore with a heavy rope in his mouth.

After the *Crazy Horse* was secured, Leka would dash off to play with the local children who had gathered in wait for him. He would run and jump and do tricks, making them squeal with laughter and delight.

Long after the games were over and they had gone home, the children would sing his praises to their parents, their voices carrying far on the warm night breeze, "Leka, Leka, Leka."

Ben busied himself on Symi. After checking in with the Coast Guard, he went to the telephone office and called his yacht agent in

Athens, to find out whether the Smiths had sent the deposit yet. If so, Ben wanted the money wired to him here, so he could buy food and drink. The agent reported that no money had come through yet. He did say, though, that he thought it would arrive by the time Ben reached the island of Kos in a couple of weeks time.

"I sure hope so," Ben said into the phone. "I'm living on bread and pasta these days."

"You'll be all right," the agent reassured him. "Just tighten your belt another notch or two."

Ben slammed the phone down and exited the office. He was so upset that he hardly paid attention to the bustling life of the harbor town as he walked back to the *Crazy Horse*.

Symi had a long, deep, horseshoe-shaped harbor. The village's houses were built on steep black hills that swept right down to the water's edge. The houses were painted in bright colors and were resplendent with flowers, grapevines and lemon trees. The harbor was a busy, noisy place. Farmers rode into town on the backs of donkeys carrying baskets of tomatoes and cucumbers. Fishermen unloaded ice-packed crates of fish, busy stevedores shouldered sacks of wheat and flour, street-sellers hawked breadsticks and packets of nuts. Small boats steamed in and out, twin-cylinder diesel engines kicking away, gah-dunk, gah-dunk.

Ben neither saw nor thought about any of that. His mind was on his personal concerns as he returned to the *Crazy Horse* and sat on its deck under the awning, a bitter, resentful taste in his mouth. Had he been a tougher and more experienced businessman he would have insisted that the Smiths put down at least half the money when the charter deal was made last spring. Instead he had settled for a promise to pay the full amount at a later date.

"You can't eat promises," Ben reminded himself.

Leka stared up worriedly, not used to seeing Ben like this, muttering darkly to himself. He licked Ben's hand, trying to cheer him up.

That afternoon Ben roused himself sufficiently enough to go ashore and walk the waterfront again, this time in search of work. With all he had learned from Lukas, maybe he could help some skipper who needed carpentry repairs or his hull scraped and painted.

But this was work most skippers did during the off-season, when their vessels were out of the water. The best Ben could find was an offer to crew on a luxury yacht. The pay was good and there would be tips on top of that, but the skipper was adamantly against having a dog on board. If Ben wanted the job, he would have to ditch Leka.

Ben stuck around Symi for a few more days, hoping some other foreign-flag boat would arrive with a prospect of employment. Asking a Greek captain for work was out of the question, as the Greeks would only hire one of their own countrymen. This was understandable. Many Greek people were out of work, especially on the islands.

Ben's luck did not change, not until he met an American, Dick Matson, who arrived on a sixteen-foot sailboat called *Old Glory*. The tiny boat was aptly named, as it was old, with faded paint, slack rigging and patched-up sails. But it had been Dick's home for the past thirteen years. In that time he had sailed up and down the Aegean, sometimes crossing over to the Turkish coast, even going as far afield as Malta and Italy.

Since Dick, who was in his late thirties, had neither a private income nor a desire to become a charter captain, Ben was curious to learn how he had managed to survive financially.

"Wait here, and I'll show you," Dick said.

He went below and fished out an easel and a tray of water paints which he proceeded to set up in a corner of the waterfront, not far from a small hotel.

"Sit down," Dick ordered. The next thing you know, he began to paint Ben's portrait. He took his time in order to attract passersby. Soon about a dozen people—some Greek, some tourists—had gathered round to watch Dick commit Ben's features to paper.

Dick was by no means a great artist, but he came up with a likeness of Ben good enough to inspire an Englishwoman to ask to have her portrait done. Then a Greek asked Dick to paint him standing in the doorway of his butcher shop. Dick kept his prices low, charging just ten dollars for each watercolor, but in the next hour he got three quick commissions and a

38

request for him to paint a larger picture of a Frenchman's motor yacht.

"I do this wherever I go," Dick confided later as they sat at a nearby taverna over glasses of ouzo and a plate of grilled octopus. "I can make about thirty dollars a day during the summer months. Outside of occasionally being hassled by the police, it's an easy and pleasant way to make a living. If you have any talent for drawing, you could do equally well at it."

Ben explained that while he had taken art classes in high school and had always liked to draw, he was a long way away from being a professional artist.

"There's only one way to find out if you can do it, and that's to do it," said the tall, lanky, boyish-looking American.

The next morning Ben did just that, switching roles with Dick. But no matter how diligently he tried, he just could not capture Dick's likeness on paper. He could get the body shape all right, but not the facial details—the planes, curves and shadings that added up to a likeness.

Dick laughed when he saw the results of Ben's first efforts. "You've given me a nose like a banana," he said. "This is so bad you couldn't even sell it as a caricature." When Ben told him he used to draw horses when young, Dick came up with a new suggestion. "Try painting a picture of your dog."

It was uncanny how switching from a human to an animal subject seemed to improve Ben's technique. No doubt his love for Leka entered into it—his hand flew, as if it had a life of its own.

"Not bad," Dick said. "Not bad at all. And I have a feeling you'll get better at it. The question is, though, will people shell out money for the portrait of a strange dog?"

The answer, as Ben found out, was only once in a while. Just one islander, a stevedore who had marveled at Leka's antics when the *Crazy Horse* was docking, paid the equivalent of five dollars for a bright little portrait of the dog.

Five dollars wasn't enough to live on, but Ben found a way to supplement that amount by painting pictures of shops and buildings. This kind of artwork was easier for him. He seemed to have a good sense of form and scale, and a feeling for human dwellings. Also, it was a lot easier to paint a stationary piece of property than a restless, inquisitive dog who kept jumping up and running off every five minutes or so.

The problem with painting buildings, though, was that few people would agree in advance to purchase the picture.

Ben had to paint the subject first, then offer it for sale. He used up a lot of paper and colors that way, though he did learn a lot about Aegean architecture. After a week of it, Ben allowed that he would have to find another way of earning his keep, if he was to survive life in the Greek islands.

Dick came up with yet another suggestion. "You're young and strong and a good swimmer," he said. "I think you could become a spearfisherman."

"I don't know anything about spearfishing," Ben replied. "It's not a sport I grew up with."

"Neither did I," Dick admitted. "But I learned it, and maybe you can, too."

"I've heard it's difficult and even a little dangerous," Ben said.

"That it is," Dick allowed. "But it's a way for you to help feed yourself—and your dog."

Ben couldn't argue with that, so the next day he got up early and, with Leka by his side, went out with Dick to see what spearfishing was all about.

The first thing Ben learned was that spearfishing had nothing to do with scuba diving. A free diver used held breath, not bottled air, while chasing fish. In Dick's case, he wore a rubber suit to keep warm and a weight belt to help him reach depths of twenty-five and thirty-five feet. His gun was a simple thing with rubber bands, like a glorified slingshot.

The technique was to paddle slowly across the surface of the sea with your flippered feet, peering down into the depths through your face mask, hoping to spot a large fish.

The Aegean was so blue and clear that one could see far down into its depths, an alluring but mysterious secret world. There weren't a lot of fish in sight, though. The Aegean did not have the exotic underwater life of the Caribbean or Red Sea. No volcanic cliffs, no schools of flashing, twisting bait fish, no kelp beds, no gaudy displays of color. The seascape here was pleasant, subdued and rather barren.

But the sunlight penetrating the ocean constantly changed the color and texture of the water. The depths of the Aegean acted like stained glass on the shafts of light, breaking them into gently shimmering spangles of gold. The sea became transformed, turned into a cathedral, a holy place of silence, awe and radiance. It almost seemed a blasphemy to be hunting for fish and lobster down here.

Dick kept at it, though, paddling slowly around and looking this way and that. Finally he spotted a large fish, a grouper, chasing a school of small fish.

The grouper sensed danger and broke off hunting and swam back to his lair, a cave beneath a tangled pile of boulders. Dick lay still, breathing quietly through his snorkel, studying the situation, deciding on his strategy. Finally he took a big gulp of air and made his dive, one hand pinching his nose to compensate against the pressure of the sea, the other proffering his gun, ready to fire.

He dove behind the rocks, attempting to keep out of the wary grouper's sight. When he reached the bottom, he flattened himself and inched around the rocks from behind. Dick moved fast only when he encountered the grouper in the mouth of the cave. Just as the startled fish backed away, Dick fired his gun, hitting the grouper with an accurate shot. Moments later he brought it up to the surface and swam with it to his dive boat, where Leka had been sitting and waiting all the while.

The fish was about a foot and a half long and must have weighed fifteen pounds. With its brown, mottled yellow body and huge, powerful head it looked like quite an adversary. Leka stared at it with wide, startled eyes.

"Catching a big fish isn't usually this easy," Dick cautioned Ben, "but now you've got an idea how it's done."

Chapter Six

The next day Ben and Leka walked to a dive shop. Ben bought himself a gun, wet suit and weight belt, and set about learning how to become a spearfisherman.

Every day he and Leka hiked out to a far beach or cove where Ben could don his suit and slip into the water, leaving Leka to explore the locale to his heart's content. When the sun heated up, Leka would take a swim and then wait for Ben, sitting and resting in the shade of an olive tree.

Ben would swim this way and that, looking for an underwater site where the big fish were. He soon discovered that Dick was right about one thing—spearfishing wasn't an easy sport. It was one thing to be able to dive, to handle the pressure on your eardrums and body, another to have the breath and presence of mind to operate in the shadowy depths.

Groupers, even the small ones, were smart and formidable, capable of defending themselves in a variety of ways. The fish had the ability to camouflage themselves and blend in with rocks and weeds when you came into view. They were also astonishingly strong, able to twist out of your grasp with one sudden, mighty shake.

It was much easier for a beginner to spear the other varieties of fish in these waters—the gray and red mullet, the sea bream, parrot fish and trigger fish. They were plentiful, but made smaller, more elusive targets. Ben missed more than he hit, but soon he began to bring in a few fish every day. He sold most of them, keeping just enough to feed Leka and himself.

Over the weeks Ben's spearfishing skills began to improve. His breath control got better, his marksmanship as well. He also started to develop a hunter's instinct, a sixth sense that told him where the fish were and which approach was best. He also found himself becoming less frightened and tentative in the sea, especially in the more forbidding depths.

One thing helping to build his confidence was that there were no sharks or barracudas to worry about in the Aegean, at least not in the relatively shallow areas where he operated. The absence of these predators meant he could concentrate on chasing fish. There was always the danger of running out of breath, but even here an instinct took over and warned him when it was time to power up to the surface for a gulp of air.

Ben found himself being in the sea every day. The deep breathing and physical exertion did wonders for body and health. He had never felt so fit and alive in his life.

It pleased him, too, knowing that if nothing else he could feed himself and Leka wherever they went. Leka had learned to enjoy eating fish almost as much as he did. Baked fish was his favorite, which he ate from his special dish, tail whipping around gleefully.

The vitamins and oils in the seafood made Leka's fur shine and his eyes gleam. His muscles seemed to grow firmer, his step became quicker and more assured. Even his bark sounded louder and bolder.

He was always thirsty, though, and lapped up copious amounts of water four or five times a day. He's not only part German shepherd, he's part camel, Ben thought.

Chapter Seven

Lukas' warning about the treacherous nature of the Aegean Sea came back to haunt Ben. It happened when the *Crazy Horse* was crossing the strait between the islands of Symi and Tilos, and a storm blew up about three in the afternoon.

It hit without warning—no darkening skies, no thunder or lightning or change of temperature. The day had dawned bright and clear, like any other summer's day in the Aegean, with the sun beating down fiercely on the little catamaran as it glided toward the island of Tilos. Ben and Leka huddled under the leecloth, in the only boat for miles around.

Suddenly the wind started to howl down out of the north. It was a hot wind, but it whipped up the sea into dirty whitecaps and began to shower the boat with spray. Ben estimated the wind's speed at Force Seven and adjusted his sails accordingly. The *Crazy Horse* flew along, rising up on the ten-foot swells and coming down with violent smacks.

47

As the afternoon went on, the wind began to back around and attack in gusts, increasing in strength all the while. The sea kept building up, too, creating waves that slammed against the cat and made it heel over. This was the *Crazy Horse's* first big challenge, and it stood up to it reasonably well, riding out the blow in plucky fashion. Some sailors believed catamarans were dangerous in rough weather, always on the verge of tipping over, especially when the sea was on the beam. But the *Crazy Horse* proved them wrong. It kept to its course, even as the sea and wind kept pounding away at it, splattering Ben with a cold, blinding spray.

Ben wished he had made a harness for Leka, to keep him from being washed over the side. But the dog, quick-witted as ever, simply wedged himself into a corner of the cockpit as tightly as he could. The only time he stood up was to occasionally shake the seawater off his wet, shivering body.

Even though the cobalt sky overhead was cloudless and the sun still shone down strongly and reflected off the sea with a white, smoky glare, the storm would not quit. The waves kept pounding away at the *Crazy Horse*, shaking its beams, crashing down on the deck with a loud roar that made Leka whimper in fear.

It got so bad that Ben decided to change course and head toward the nearest speck of land, a tiny island about two nautical miles to the west. Wearing a life jacket, Ben had to use all his strength to keep the *Crazy Horse* on target. He had unfurled a small, heavy staysail, but even with that improvement, it was a struggle to keep the cat going. Ben felt apprehensive, but he was a long way from panicking. For all its creaking and shuddering, the *Crazy Horse* still responded well to his touch. He had a good feeling about the boat even as it was being assaulted by the sea. Small and stubby as the cat was, it had been built well and was managing to stand up to this sudden, nasty blow.

Still, it was unnerving to be out at sea all alone, with no radio to call for help if needed. How insignificant he and Leka and the *Crazy Horse* were, piddling little objects in a vast, wild, uncaring universe. They were on their own, at the mercy of the elements, whether they liked it or not.

When they finally reached the island, Ben was disappointed to discover there was no harbor secure enough to anchor in. The island was even too small to offer up any wind protection, if only because the storm had become circular, with the wind swirling this way and that, reversing itself in eggbeater fashion.

All Ben could find was an indentation in the gray, pock-marked cliffs, one just large enough to permit the *Crazy Horse* to enter and take cover behind a high, spiral-shaped rock.

Ben put out lines and tried to steady the *Crazy Horse* in one position behind the rock, but the storm was treacherous and kept changing direction, forcing him to keep moving the boat around.

It meant that Ben could not rest. He had to be ready at all times to jump ashore and adjust the lines to cope with the newly surging sea. Sometimes he moved the cat a few feet to port, other times to starboard, in an attempt to stay shielded behind the rock. He felt like a kid crouched behind a tree, trying to avoid being seen in a game of hide-and-seek.

It went on like that. Ben barely had time to go below to feed himself and Leka. He kept awake at night by drinking coffee and talking to Leka, who stayed by his side, ducking every time a monster wave crashed against the rock and sent dark, cold seawater cascading down on them. The dog was terrified but tried his best not to show it.

Normally a summer storm like this lasted only a few hours, but this one would not obey any of the rules. It blew all through the night and then through the next day, increasing in intensity, howling louder and louder. Pretty soon another day and night had gone by, with no letup in sight. Ben slept sitting up in half hour increments, not wanting to be caught unawares by the treacherous currents. Though his body ached with fatigue, and he was soaked through and through, he could not afford to let his guard down. One mistake in positioning the *Crazy Horse* and the boat would be smashed to pieces against the rock.

Leka again showed what a good guard dog he was. If Ben fell into a deep sleep at a dangerous time, he would bark loudly and tug at Ben's pants' leg, not quitting until Ben woke and stumbled across the deck to reposition the lines. Sometimes Ben didn't even know he was awake, doing the work by instinct and habit.

In his conscious moments, Ben would marvel at the whole thing. Here was this horrible, unending storm raging on, yet the days were still bright and warm, the nights clear and star-filled. It was as if the sea had mind of its own and refused to have anything to do with the rest of the elements.

As time went on a new problem presented itself—their food and water began to run out. Ben regretted not having stocked more provisions, but it just hadn't seemed necessary when he had started the cruise, not when you were always within sight and reach of another island.

Even with rationing, supplies dwindled to next to nothing, especially their water. Soon Ben could pour only a few drops into Leka's dish, which the dog lapped up instantly, looking up thirstily for more.

Ben's mouth was so cracked and dry that he could hardly speak. "No more left," he mumbled apologetically as he showed Leka the empty bottle. "Our fresh water is all gone."

Leka whimpered and slunk off to a corner of the cockpit, where he brooded for some time, pink tongue drooping out of his parched mouth. Finally he raised himself and came over to Ben, making urgent noises in his throat. Assuming he needed to relieve himself, Ben lifted him up and carefully placed him on shore.

Leka picked his way up a narrow, slippery

ledge until he reached the top of the cliffs. With the waves thudding away noisily below, he turned and disappeared from view.

Leka did not return to the *Crazy Horse* for the longest time. Ben found himself beginning to get worried. Could Leka have got lost? Had he slipped off the cliff and tumbled into the sea while trying to return?

Ben was about to go ashore to look for him when the dog appeared at the top of the bluff. Instead of picking his way down, he stood there and barked at Ben, again and again.

Ben realized that Leka was trying to communicate with him about something urgent. Obediently, he jumped from the boat to the ledge and clambered up the trail.

It was forbidding up top, all dark, jagged rocks and patches of hard clay. The footing was slick and tricky, thanks to the sea spray that was splattering everything in sight. There was a narrow path, though, and Leka led Ben down it to where a small Greek Orthodox chapel stood. It had been built with stones and chunks of shale, no doubt by a grateful seafarer, who, like Ben, had once found shelter here in a storm.

Some stones had been piled up beside the chapel. Leka stopped and turned to Ben, his body quivering with excitement and anticipation. The stones were holding down a wooden cover. Ben dropped to his knees and removed the stones, one by one. Then he lifted the cover and peered down into a deep, dim shaft. Picking up a pebble, he tossed it into the dimness.

Moments later, he heard a splash.

Ben entered the chapel and looked around. There was a whitewashed altar, a homemade wooden crucifix, and a couple of crudely painted icons, a batch of beeswax candles, an old cot with a blanket and a pillow—and a bucket on a rope.

After lowering the bucket into the shaft, Ben hauled it up, hand over hand, wondering what it would bring—fresh, drinkable liquid or just a load of smelly seawater?

The answer was there in the clear, silvery substance that filled the bucket. All it took was one taste for Ben to realize how pure the water was, having bubbled up from an underground spring fed by winter rains.

Both he and Leka drank their fill, taking turns at plunging their faces into the bucket and slurping the cool, sweet-tasting water to their heart's content.

Chapter Eight

From that time on, Leka was no longer just a pet, a lovable creature whose company Ben enjoyed. Having learned just how special Leka was, Ben treated him as he would a brother, a soulmate. Leka reciprocated with deep feelings of his own, never leaving Ben's side unless ordered to. When they were together they seemed to understand each other's thoughts and needs. All it took was a look, a cock of the head, a word or two, for communication to be achieved.

Being with each other made them both happy. Ben's happiness was made more complete by the days that followed the brush with death off the coast of Symi. As awful and dangerous as the Aegean had been, it was benevolent and tranquil now, with breezes that were perfect for sailing and would push the *Crazy Horse* along at a swift, exhilarating clip.

Temperatures were warm but not oppressive, the sky was as blue as butterfly's wings. To sail the Aegean like this was to feel one's heart sinking into paradise. Ben felt that everything his parents had dreamed of was coming true—here he was, sitting at the helm of his own boat, swiftly hurling along over the waves, sailing far, sailing free. That he had a wonder dog by his side was the whipped cream on his cake.

Underneath his happiness, though, was a twinge of sadness. Why couldn't his parents be here to enjoy this perfect day at sea? He could just picture them on the *Crazy Horse*, his father standing by the tiller, steering it with a leg as he gazed out over the sea, watching the way the wind filled the sails and ruffled the surface of the water. His father usually wore shorts and a cap while at sea, liking the feeling of the sun on his deeply tanned, muscular body. Ben's mother, though, had fair skin and never went on deck without a wide-brimmed straw hat and long sleeves. She loved to curl up under the leecloth and read one book after another while sailing, looking up from the page only to flash Ben a warm, loving smile.

Ben's eyes filled with tears as he thought of his parents and realized how much he missed them. At times like this, life could really hurt.

The Aegean became clearer and bluer as the days went by, and Ben couldn't wait to pull into a cove and drop anchor, freeing him to put on his wetsuit and go underwater again. Leka swam out to sea with him and paddled around in circles while Ben searched for fish. When he became chilled, Leka headed to shore and rolled around in the hot sand to warm up.

After that, he'd curl up under a shady tree for one of his beloved naps.

The sea was much warmer now, though when you pushed down twenty or thirty feet the temperature dropped considerably and made wearing a wetsuit necessary. It was important to be warm and relaxed while stalking fish. The less commotion you made, the better chance you had of surprising the big ones, some of whom liked to laze around on the bottom once they had eaten their fill of smaller fish. Once Ben had even speared a grouper that was taking a nap on a big, black sponge!

The clarity of the Aegean never ceased to amaze him. Though there were often strong currents swirling around in the depths, they rarely churned up the sandy bottom sufficiently to obscure his vision. Ben could lie on the surface, breathing quietly through his snorkel, and see everything beneath him—the schools of tiny silver fish flicking about, the odd parrot fish or two nibbling on the plants that grew beside the rocks and boulders, the dark caves in the sides of cliffs where the big fish lurked.

The more he dived the better he learned the ways of the creatures occupying the depths. One way of spotting a grouper's lair was to look out for a pack of tiny black fish—in Greek they were called bouboulitsa—hanging about a rock. If they jumped back suddenly, it meant a big fish had made a threatening move at them. To find the spineless Aegean lobster called caravida, you looked up, not straight ahead, when you peered into a cave. Caravides clung upside down on the roofs of caves, using their sharp, purple-tinged claws to hold on tightly until night came, and it was safe for them to venture out in search of food.

As Ben became a better hunter, he also became better conditioned, able to hold his breath for as much as two minutes and to dive into the depths where the shafts of sunlight did not reach and all was dark and mysterious. Down here he used an underwater flashlight to illuminate the caves and holes.

The deep diving served to sharpen his eyesight as well. He could now spot a camouflaged octopus from twenty feet away, or a fat, black-tipped sea bream as it slipped into a batch of weeds and hid there. He also learned to identify the oysters that grew wild in the Aegean. Mostly they were attached to the sides of rocks and reefs, so firmly that it took a special, heavy-duty knife to pry them loose. It sometimes took Ben half a dozen dives to do the job. But the work was worth it, because these shellfish were incredibly tasty and fetched a handsome price from the restaurants.

By bringing in fish, lobster and shellfish, Ben found he was able to support himself as he slowly worked his way through the Aegean toward his ultimate destination of Athens, where he was to pick up the Smiths. He and Leka could eat well too—sometimes Ben traded fish for meat, the finest cuts. He was also able to buy cans of dog food for an emergency, and to stock up on fruit and vegetables for himself. You didn't need fancy food to eat well in the Aegean, if only because the ingredients were so fresh and delicious—huge, fat tomatoes, cucumbers and watermelon just off the vine, crusty bread right out of the oven, feta cheese and yogurt made by shepherds who brought their goods to market every morning.

Living and sailing on the *Crazy Horse* also helped sharpen Ben's feeling of well-being. Breathing clean air, being baked brown by the sun, diving every day—all these things did wonders for him. All his senses were sharpened, especially his sense of taste. Food seemed to taste better. Just a little sea-salt sprinkled on his Greek salad brought out all kinds of subtle flavors. It must have been the same for Leka, because he ate with gusto these days and looked healthier and happier all the time, especially when he was playing or doing something with Ben.

Ben couldn't get over how well things were going. He was even improving as an artist! He would never make the world forget about Picasso and Van Gogh, but his still-lifes and portraits weren't bad, not in this market anyway, which, let's face it, wasn't all that discriminating. The tourists who bought his stuff just wanted to take home a pleasant souvenir of their stay in the islands.

Ben's town-studies and renderings of houses and shops were still better than his portraits—except when it came to Leka. He couldn't exactly explain why his hand grew more subtle and skillful when he drew or painted his sidekick. Whatever the reason, though, one thing was certain—his studies of Leka were striking and unusual, even powerful.

This wasn't just the vain artist talking. Almost everyone who came to look at Ben's artwork—he had hung a sign on the boat, "The *Crazy Horse* Gallery"—agreed that the Leka portraits were superb. They were so taken with them that he found he could sell them easily, even when he raised the price to twenty-five dollars or more.

More validation came a week later, when the *Crazy Horse* touched down at a flyspeck island called Nisyros. One of Greece's two volcanic islands (the other was Santorini), Nisyros was shaped like an upside-down ice cream cone. The origin of the island was attributed to Polyvotis, a giant who incurred the wrath of the sea god Poseidon, who tore off a chunk of nearby Kos and hurled it on top of Polyvotis when he attempted to swim away. This became the island of Nisyros, and the miserable Polyvotis, pinned underneath, eternally groaned and fumed, unable to escape.

Ben put in at the island's main town of Mandraki, which was packed with two-story white houses, serpentine streets, lush gardens and hilltop monasteries. The dock was close to the post and telephone offices, but Ben chose to stay here only one night. It was the noise that drove him away. Every five or six hours a huge ferryboat would arrive with horns blaring. It would drop anchor, discharge passengers and freight, and take off as loudly and quickly as it had come.

Ben moved the *Crazy Horse* around to the eastern side of the island where the fishing village of Pali offered a small, protected harbor. Pali was silent and peaceful. Ben and Leka were able to make friends with the dozen-odd fishermen who lived here. There was a pleasant seafront taverna called Hellenis, which was run by a couple named Manoli and Paraskevi. Manoli, who was originally from the island of Crete, kept flocks of sheep and goats, which meant there would always be good meat to eat. Manoli reminded Ben of Lukas—though he was much younger than the master carpenter, he had the same big white moustache and wise airs.

Manoli also brought out a violin when the mood was on him, and that brought villagers from near and far to hear him play. Soon, inspired by the ouzo and wine poured by Paraskevi, they began to sing along with him, calling up the folk songs from their youth. Then tables and chairs would be pushed aside to make room, and the dancing would begin, the intricate, rhythmic dances of the islands. Sometimes only men danced, arms linked, heads bowed, expressions grave and concentrated. Then the women joined them, and the dances became lighter, more joyous and freewheeling. The dancing continued for hours.

These islanders knew how to entertain themselves without the help of television shows or movies. Everyone took part in these impromptu parties. Those too old or ill to dance joined in the singing. Those who couldn't sing simply clapped hands along with the music. It was a communal and spontaneous event, one that lifted everyone's spirits and made them feel glad to be alive, especially when the moon came up over the village and cast a magical, silvery glow over everything.

Manoli and Paraskevi had two sons about Ben's age, and they became good pals. They took Ben and Leka up to see the caldera, a huge hole in the ground where a volcano had erupted with the force of an H-bomb many thousands of years ago. Today the caldera was a tourist attraction. Busloads of visitors were brought up here daily to gawk at its moonscape-like craters and boulders. The caldera still had some fire in its belly—sulphuric steam leaked from yellow-stained cracks and holes, emitting a smell like rotten eggs. Leka recoiled when he sniffed the air, shooting Ben a look of horror and disbelief. Then he turned and raced up the path, putting lots of distance between him and the stench.

Ben continued to look around, though. There were geo-thermal pools of water, and he could feel the heat and turmoil of the volcano through the soles of his shoes. He also met some engineers who were studying ways that all this pent-up energy could be tapped to provide electrical power to the island.

Later, the boys took Ben and Leka to visit Nisyros' other two villages, Nikia and Emborio, which sat on opposite hilltops overlooking the

caldera. These villages were as small and dra-
matically situated as eagle's nests, but they
were near-empty, their inhabitants having left
to find work in Mandraki or on nearby Kos.
Ben and Leka enjoyed wandering around and
investigating back streets and chatting with
the occasional villager they met in the streets.

Nisyros was surprisingly green and fertile,
thanks to the hot, sulphuric waters bubbling
away beneath the island's surface. You couldn't
drink these waters, but they did feed the roots
of the fruit trees covering the hillsides and
fields. Nisyros was famous for its figs, some of
which were big as handballs when ripe. Ben
and his friends picked figs together, filling
basket after basket of the sweet, succulent
green and black fruit in less than an hour.

Leka went with them wherever they ex-
plored, hiking round the town, scurrying up
the narrow steps of the Monastery of Panagia
Spiliana, named after the island's patron saint.
When the sun became too hot, they would all
return to the sea and cool off in the hard-run-
ning, choppy surf. Ben would then break out
his speargun and go hunting for fish.

All this physical activity tired them out by
late afternoon, Leka in particular. He would
find a bit of shade on the quay where the *Crazy Horse* was moored and curl up for a nap.
Ben used that time to sketch him—it was the
only time Leka would hold still.

Ben was so deeply absorbed in his work that
he didn't hear the approach of the person who
came up behind him and said, "I love your

work."

Startled, Ben turned and encountered a tall, handsome, middle-aged woman who was wearing a brightly-colored summer dress and a big, floppy bonnet. Her voice was deep and warm and sounded lightly British. She had long, wavy hair the color of black figs and had a young boy by her side who appeared to be about nine or ten years old.

The woman said she was Greek but had been educated in Britain, where she had met her husband, a lawyer who represented several Greek shipowners based in London. Her name was Zoe Kondylis-Bennet, and she ran a small art gallery on the island of Kos during the summer. Her son's name was Nikos, and he loved dogs. Nikos took Leka off to play. It didn't take long for Leka and the small, dark-haired boy to become the best of friends.

Over coffee, Zoe and Ben had a chat. "I've built up a rather nice clientele over the years and think I could sell your sketches and paintings for a lot more than you're getting now," she said.

"You really think so?" Ben asked in disbelief. "I've never thought of myself as a professional painter."

"Well, you are one, at least where the likenesses of Leka are concerned," Zoe replied. "They show depth, feeling and sensitivity. Dog pictures are always commercial, but yours are special because they're more than just sentimental renderings. They capture a unique animal in a loving way."

In the face of such flattery, Ben could not resist Zoe's offer to become his exclusive representative. She wanted to start things off with a one-man show at the gallery. If that proved successful, she would contract with him for a steady stream of work, guaranteeing to buy his entire output for the next year.

"I might even be able to put together a book of your sketches," she continued. "I'd sell the book through a mail-order campaign. I believe we could do rather well with it," she said. "We might even make a bit of lolly."

A bit of lolly—British for money.

Ben couldn't help laughing at the way Zoe spoke. She looked so Greek with her deep-black hair and eyes and her olive skin—yet sounded so upper-class British. She was an impressive woman, though. She had an air of competency and assuredness about her. He felt she would do whatever she said she would and that he could trust her where business and money were concerned. Besides, she was such good fun to be with. She knew Greece well and loved its food, music and people.

Nikos was a typical Greek island kid. He lived in shorts and a t-shirt, went around barefoot most of the time, and was a skilled swimmer and diver. Without a wet suit or weights, he could kick down over twenty feet with ease. "I'm not keen on shooting fish," he told Ben, "but I do like to hunt for shells and things."

"Things?"

Nikos' grin showed the gaps in his teeth. "What I mostly do is patrol the waters around the tourist beaches. You'd be amazed what people lose while swimming. Just this summer alone I've found a lot of jewelry like wristwatches, bracelets and ankle chains."

"What else?"

"Oh, lots of sunglasses. Dozens of them, really."

"Congratulations. You're the salvage king of the Greek islands! What's the best thing you ever found underwater?"

Nikos grinned again. "You probably wouldn't believe me."

"Try me."

"A Rolex watch. Do you know how much it's worth?"

"I have no idea."

"About five thousand dollars."

Ben put his head back and laughed. Here he was, knocking himself out to catch fish which he could sell for a few dollars while this little squirt became rich with one simple dive.

Leka liked Nikos as much as Ben did. Since the boy had a dog of his own, he was comfortable around Leka and knew how to handle him. Leka was so smitten with Nikos that he hardly paid much attention to Ben that night.

For the first time ever Ben felt peeved with Leka. Later he realized there was a better word for it—jealous.

Imagine that, he said to himself. You are jealous of a dog. Not a girlfriend. Not a brother or sister—a *dog*. He was learning something about himself every day.

65

Chapter Nine

Zoe's gallery was located in the center of Kos, right on Akti Miaouli, the city's main waterfront street. The tourists and locals liked to take their evening strolls there, especially when the sun was setting, a fiery red ball that slipped down behind the horizon and lit the sky spectacularly in tints of crimson, pink and magenta. Not only were there several restaurants serving tasty food and drink but dozens of shops offering jewelry, clothing and trinkets.

As night fell, the smell of meat and fish being grilled was enticing, as was the sight of fishing boats and private yachts riding at anchor. On every corner men sold peanuts and Asian sweets from wooden carts lit by the white light of pump-up lanterns. Music rang from outdoor jukeboxes, the latest pop hits from Athens. Over everything curved a black sky showing glittering stars and an enormous half moon.

Kos reminded Ben of Rhodes. It even had an Old Town built by the Crusaders, though it

was much smaller and less intact, having suf-
fered damage from earthquakes and wars
over the centuries. But it was still possible to
visit the Castle of the Knights of St. John and
to walk around the fortress embankments,
built in medieval times by the Crusaders when
they came down from Europe to battle the sol-
diers of the Ottoman Empire. The Ottoman
Empire was based just twenty miles away, in
the mountains of Turkey. The stones of the Old
Town were steeped in history and atmosphere.

Kos was also famous as the birthplace of
Hippocrates, the father of medicine, who lived
there in the fifth-century BC and was the first
to realize that diseases were not punishments
sent from God, but had natural causes.

Hippocrates was the first to suggest that
healers should discover as much as possible
about each patient and his symptoms before
making a diagnosis. He founded a school in
the village of Asklipion where he taught pu-
pils a wholesome medicine based on waters,
special diets, herbal remedies and relaxation.
He also devised a standard of medical ethics
incorporated in the Hippocratic Oath taken by
doctors to this day. Ben, with Leka by his side,
was thrilled to stand on the site where all this
had taken place.

Zoe's gallery was called Mythos. A large,
white-washed, high-ceilinged room, it was divided into three sections, one of which featured
classic Greek painters, another of which concentrated on modern works by both Greek and
foreign artists. The third section offered lesser

priced items such as prints, sketches, posters and lithographs.

"These are popular with people who don't have much money and buy art just occasionally," Zoe explained.

In order to supply Zoe with enough work to see her through the rest of the summer, Ben stayed put for the next ten days and concentrated on turning out sketches and watercolors of Leka.

To make it easier for Ben to work, Zoe gave him a back room at the gallery which she had set aside for visiting artists. It had a skylight as well as artificial light, a work table, various easels and cabinets, a small hot plate and refrigerator, and a couch ideal for reading and resting.

Leka liked the room as much as Ben did, if only because he could be visited by Nikos and his dog, an Irish setter named Hector, named after the mythical Trojan hero killed by Achilles. Hector had a red, silky coat and long, thick ears that hung down close to his head. He was an exuberant dog with much joy of life who always wanted to romp and have fun, to the point of becoming overexcited and annoying. Nikos always had to calm him down.

It took Leka several days to get used to having another dog as a friend, but fortunately Hector, who had been raised and trained in England, was patient and companionable. As he was older and more experienced, Hector took the lead in building the friendship. He taught Leka how to play in rough and tumble fashion, and also introduced him to the city of Kos.

Ben wasn't happy about Leka taking off without him and poking around in a strange environment, but Zoe assured him that Nikos knew all the dangers out there and would look after both dogs. Ben also felt confident that the inhabitants of Kos would protect Leka as best they could, if only because they liked him so much.

Wherever Leka went, be it along the waterfront or across the main square, Platia Eleftheria, people would call out to him, "Yassou, Leka!" It was like saying "Hi" or "How are you?"

There were many good things for dogs to do in Kos, many different kinds of places to visit and investigate, starting with the central market with its outdoor stalls offering food of every kind. Its vendors would shout, "Fresh swordfish!" and "Get your lamb here!" and "Loukoumia, try this loukoumia, it's as sweet as a Sultana's kiss!" Nikos knew all these hawkers and vendors. They called his name and tossed Hector scraps of meat and tried to pet him.

Nikos was also fond of the Old Town with its cubbyhole shops where artisans made shoes and sandals or repaired iron and copper pots or built tables and cabinets. Few tourists came here but the atmosphere was striking—dark, narrow, cobbled streets and houses with big, high wooden doors decorated with markings from the Crusader days. It was like going back in time and visiting another world to walk through the Old Town and pass by a Turkish mosque with its slender, graceful minaret. There was also a shop which made its own ice cream and pastries. The owner always gave Nikos an extra amount of sweets when he served him.

As for Leka, he liked the waterfront areas best, especially the boatyard if only because it reminded him of Petros', the place where he had met Ben and Lukas. There was the same sprawl and mess, the boats scattered every which way on the beach, the smell of woodchips and paint, the sound of hammering, sawing and scraping filling the air. It was like home, especially on a day like this with the smoky sunlight pouring down, bringing out the vivid colors of the boats and sea. While Nikos snorkeled at a nearby beach, searching for more jewelry and sunglasses, Leka and Hector scampered around in the yard, sniffing out bits of old canvas and wood, rolling around and wrestling in the sand, cleaning themselves with a quick dip in the softly rolling surf.

Nikos also took the dogs to see the various boats and ships that called in at Kos—the trawlers, freighters, sponge-diving caiques and inter-island ferries. Once in a while a huge cruise ship dropped anchor, a massive, four-story-high vessel that carried a thousand tourists and was met by a swarm of people, not just Coast Guard but stevedores, sailors, bus and taxi drivers, porters, vendors and travel agents. This was where Nikos sold many of the items he had salvaged over the summer.

In a far corner of the waterfront was the marina where the smaller boats like *Crazy Horse* were moored. Leka took Nikos and Hector aboard the catamaran, showing them the bridgedeck, the cockpit, the salon, galley and berths below. Then the three of them went ashore, with the dogs racing off and giving a nearby cat the scare of its life.

Everywhere they went they were accompanied with the cry, "Yassou, Leka! Yassou!"

Next they stopped by a waterfront bar called "The Sundowner," where the Australian owner always put out a dish of water for Leka. "Watch this," he'd tell his patrons whenever an incoming yacht approached.

"Fetch," he'd say to Leka. "Fetch the forward line."

Leka immediately stepped to the edge of the dock and threw himself fearlessly into the sea, sticking his snout up when he surfaced and paddling out to the boat at full speed.

"Toss it!" the Australian would then call out to the skipper. "Toss him your line!"

It took the disbelieving skipper a few minutes to obey, but when he did Leka would seize the wet, thick rope in his jaws and start back to the dock, legs flailing away to keep him moving. When he reached the dock he'd tread water with all his might, waiting for someone to haul the rope up with a boathook.

Then the familiar cry would go up around the waterfront: "Bravo, Leka, bravo!"

It took Hector a week to summon up the nerve to imitate Leka. Hector was neither as used to the sea nor as courageous as Leka was, being a house dog by training, but he couldn't let Leka win all the praise and attention. Pretty soon, whenever Leka leapt in the sea to retrieve a line, he was followed by a flying ball of red fur with long floppy ears.

When Zoe felt she had enough work from Ben to keep her stocked, she and her husband Mark gave him a surprise party. They had dinner at Kos' best restaurant and invited a few of the gallery's other artists to celebrate with them later at a nightclub known for its bouzouki music and spirited dancing.

Mark might have been a lawyer and upright citizen, but the slim, sandy-haired Englishman also knew how to relax and have a good time. He danced one Greek dance after another, sometimes with Zoe and a group of friends, other times by himself, doing the zeybekiko, a highly individualistic dance involving slow, deliberate steps broken up with sudden leaps, turns and splits, punctuated with snaps of fingers and whacks of heels.

"How can I learn to dance like that?" Ben asked him.

"It's easy," was Mark's reply. "just marry a Greek woman."

Joining them at the table was Telly Platanos, a skilled and successful Greek portrait-painter. He had taken Ben under his wing and given him the first professional art lessons of his life. Thanks to Telly, Ben's work improved since coming to Kos. His technique was defter and assured, his understanding of composition and scale more developed and precise. He also learned how to paint with oils.

Best of all, Telly backed up Zoe's belief in Ben's work. "I think some of his drawings of Leka are excellent," he told her. "It makes good sense to publish them in a book."

Zoe talked it over with Mark and decided to go ahead immediately with the project, arranging to meet Ben in Athens, when he arrived for his charter with the Smiths. With the help of a fine-arts printer, she planned to turn them into a handsome volume which she'd offer for sale in Greece and abroad.

Ben left the nightclub feeling as good as he had ever felt in his life. Not only did he have a patron who liked his work and was willing to risk her own money to publish it, he had also earned the respect and admiration of a professional like Telly. It gave him a newfound confidence and buoyancy.

Ben's step was jaunty, and he was humming one of the bouzouki tunes when he reached the *Crazy Horse*. As soon as he boarded the cat, he went to where Leka slept, lacking only a glimpse of the dog to make his happiness complete.

What greeted him, though, was a sight that served to unnerve him. The curled-up mound of rope was in its place, but not Leka.

Ben assumed that, because the night was chilly and damp, Leka had gone down below to sleep. He searched the salon, then the berths in the twin hulls.

Nothing.

Ben went ashore and phoned Zoe, thinking that perhaps Leka had decided to stay the night with Nikos and Hector. But she reported that she had no idea where his dog was.

Ben walked around the marina, calling Leka's name, waiting for his familiar bark to sound in reply. Instead there was only the sound of the wind rattling around in the rigging of the boats moored there. As the waves kept slapping against the shore, he heard his own voice crying out, again and again, "Leka, where are you? Leka, where are you?"

Chapter Ten

The man who had kidnapped Leka was named Vasili Pappas. He had been sitting on the waterfront over a coffee when Leka did his trick with the line. Unlike the other onlookers, who had good-naturedly cheered the dog, Vasili had said nothing, if only because he was not a man of good cheer.

Vasili had spent much of his life in prison. His father was a professional thief and had trained him to follow in his footsteps. The trouble was, neither of them was terribly good at what he did. They were always getting caught.

Vasili, who was only thirty years old, had already spent more than fifteen years in one institution or another, beginning in reform school when he was young and going on to adult places of detention. With a record like that, it was hard for him to get a job, which meant he had to start stealing again to stay alive.

On this particular day he had sat for hours on the waterfront, trying to figure out his next move. Vasili, a dour, dark-haired man whose arms were covered with tattoos, had been thinking of possibly breaking into a shop that night. Thus, he didn't pay much attention to Leka, not until the men around him started speaking of his other exploits, such as his prowess as a sheep dog.

That triggered off something in Vasili's mind. He had a cousin who was a shepherd. Yorgos wasn't a thief, but he wasn't above buying stolen items from him, things like radios and whiskey. Vasili was willing to bet that Yorgos would not only be glad to have a dog like Leka but would pay good money for him.

So that night Vasili returned to the marina, this time behind the wheel of a car he had rented. He sat in darkness far away from the tavernas and bright lights, smoking one cigarette after another as he watched the *Crazy Horse*. Then, when he saw Leka come trotting back to the catamaran by himself, he got out of the car and called his name, trying to make his voice sound friendly. Leka stopped and looked his way, a bit warily. Vasili set a bowl filled with water down on the dock.

"Ella tho," he muttered to him in Greek. "Come here. Echo nero," he added. "I have water." Leka, who was always thirsty, edged closer.

"Ella, ella," Vasily urged. "Isthe kalos skilos. You're such a good dog."

Leka took a few more steps. Then, deciding to trust Vasili's soft, friendly words, he started lapping up the cool, welcome water.

Vasili petted Leka as he drank, trying to get him used to his touch. That made Leka relax his guard a little more. Vasili kept rubbing the thick fur on Leka's back and murmuring, "Good dog, good dog," only to suddenly slip a loop of rope around Leka's neck and pull it tight.

Leka immediately let out a howl and started to fight back, but Vasili yanked harder and picked up Leka like a side of beef and tossed him into the trunk of his car, slamming the lid shut on him.

Then Vasili sped out of the city and into the interior of the island, toward Oromedon, Kos' highest mountain. Leka kept barking and trying to get out, but to no avail. Vasili found the road to the village of Asphendiou, from there switching to a narrow dirt road that was pocked with holes and littered with rocks and shale. He followed it high up into the mountain, turning this way and that as the road curled round the peak of Oromedon. It was black and wild up there, with a wind that howled so loudly that not even Vasili could hear Leka's cries.

The car skidded and bounced, but Vasili kept racing toward the stone hut where Orgos lived alone all summer long while tending his sheep and goats.

Chapter Eleven

Tracking down a missing dog proved to be a lot harder than Ben had imagined. Even though it was obvious that Leka had been stolen, the police refused to get involved. "Dogs are not our business," they said, leaving it at that.

Since there was no animal rights organization on Kos, Ben had nowhere to turn except to friends. They did what they could, helping him to print a handbill which they tacked up around town, advertising for Leka's whereabouts. When the islanders saw it they commiserated with Ben, wishing him luck and promising to keep an eye out for his dog.

"What a shame you've lost him," one of them said. "He's such a wonderful animal. I hope nothing bad has happened to him."

When no word of Leka turned up, Ben began visiting other parts of the island, where he put handbills up and asked everyone he met if they knew anything. Always the identical answer came back, "I'm sorry, my friend, but I haven't seen your dog around here."

A week went by. Ben spent all his time looking for Leka, even though he should have taken to the sea again to reach Athens in time to pick up the Smiths. Although they still hadn't sent the deposit money, they had at least wired a message saying it would soon be coming.

Ben stopped spearfishing and sketching, having lost all heart for those endeavors. He also lost his appetite and was unable to sleep more than a few hours at night.

Zoe, Mark and Nikos became worried about him, but they were powerless to do anything about finding Leka. Whoever had stolen him had done a good job of covering his tracks and hiding the dog from sight—that is, if he were still alive.

Ben hated to think such thoughts. It didn't stand to reason that anyone would kidnap Leka with the intention of killing him. Chances are, it was a shepherd who had snatched him, if only because Leka was so skilled at handling sheep and goats. But at this time of year the shepherds and their flocks lived high up in the mountains, in inaccessible huts and caves. It would take Ben months to go from place to place in search of Leka—and even then he might not find him.

Reluctantly, Ben gave up the hunt and tried to get on with his life. He managed to make some minor repairs on the catamaran, but he just could not summon up the energy or desire to do anything that required serious exertion. He even tried to make sketches of Hector and

Nikos, but his hand was so heavy and clumsy that he ripped up the results.

He did manage to start spearfishing again, though, if only to put fresh food on the table. Having bought the boy a wetsuit for his birthday, Ben took Nikos out with him, not to fish but to watch and learn. But things seemed to go wrong almost every day.

First, Ben's favorite gun developed problems, a malfunctioning in the trigger mechanism. No sooner did he fix it than he broke a spear tip by striking a rock with an errant shot. It took days to find a machinist who could repair the broken tip and restore it to working order.

The incident made Ben realize that he should carry an extra spear gun with him when he went out fishing. Taking an inner tube made for a motor scooter, he turned it into a float that could be towed behind on the end of a long line. He also attached a small net to the float in which he could stash the lobsters, small fish and oysters he found in the depths.

But, as he told Nikos, all the extra equipment in the world could not help you when your luck has turned bad.

Awful things kept happening. One time he shot a big grouper—it must have been a fifteen-pounder—only to have it summon up all of its strength and wrench out of his hands. Another time he speared an even bigger fish only to see the line break and the fish take off for the deep with his spear still dangling from its side.

This was the painful, maddening side of spearfishing—a sport, Ben was beginning to realize, that was best-suited for people who liked to suffer.

As if to hammer the point home, one of his flippers broke just as he was powering himself to the surface with a five-pound trigger fish in his hands, making the ascent's last fifteen feet agonizingly difficult and dangerous. Fortunately, Nikos was there to dive down and help pull him to the surface.

"I could see you struggling," Nikos said. "I was scared that you were drowning."

"It wasn't as bad as it looked," Ben said. "But I'm still glad you gave me a hand."

All of those things contrived to put Ben into a low mood. His life, which seemed so perfect and fulfilling just a few weeks ago, had turned sour.

Up on his mountain peak, Leka was just as unhappy. His new master Yorgas was a silent, hostile man with ice-pick eyes. In his sheepskin jacket and leggings, he resembled one of the animals in his flock. Glad as he was to buy Leka from Vasili, he never gave the dog a kind word or showed him a moment of affection. Nor did he ever remove the rope from around his neck.

"You're not going anywhere," he told the dog. "You'll stay here till I've trained you to obey me."

Yorgos' way of training Leka was to hit him with a stick every time he gave an order. "Ka'tse," he'd snarl, "Sit!" And lash out angrily if Leka didn't obey him in an instant.

Hurting and afraid, Leka also lost his appetite. He wasn't getting much exercise anyway, tethered as he was by the rope to a stake in the ground. He sat pretty much in one spot all day, moving around only to escape the heat of the sun or the force of the wind. Since Yorgos never washed him, his fur became caked with mud and thistles, and one of his eyes became infected and swollen.

Finally, Leka came to the realization that no one, neither Ben nor Hector nor Nikos, could save him. If his life were going to change, he would have to take action himself.

That night, when Yorgos went to his hut and stretched out on a pile of straw, Leka began to chew on his rope. The rope was old and thick, almost as hard as steel. But he kept chewing away at it, working on the same spot.

Soon his jaws began to ache but he would not allow himself to stop. If he were going to escape, he had to gnaw through the rope before Yorgos woke at dawn. It meant staying up all night, fighting through his fatigue and pain—pain that became excruciating as the hours went by and his jaws ground away steadily, relentlessly. The only time Leka stopped was when the pain became so intense that he had to give a cry or moan. Then he would return to his work.

What kept him going was the thought of freedom, of being able to flee from here and return to Ben and the *Crazy Horse*. That's all he kept in mind as he chewed away on his restraint, stomach recoiling at its foul taste. It wasn't until dawn came up in the sky, a streak of soft, violet light that Leka finally succeeded in chewing through the rope. Quickly, he got to his feet and raced as fast as he could down the side of the mountain, the rope still tied to his neck dragging behind him.

Leka picked his way down, sticking to the trails. Trouble was, there were dozens of trails, some of which looked as if they were heading down toward Asphendiou, only to take a sharp turn and start uphill again. Leka had to call on all his instincts to find the right way home. The rocks underfoot were sharp and hurt his feet, and as the sun came up the temperature began to soar.

He continued to push on, though, pausing only to take a drink of water from a creek or basin. Panting heavily, with his tongue drooping from his bleeding mouth, he felt better when the slope began to level off, and he came upon groves of olive trees and fields of wheat. On and on he pushed, with only one goal in mind—to find his way back to Ben and the *Crazy Horse*.

Once he reached the city of Kos, it became easier for him, especially when he picked up Hector's scent to help guide him. It was morning, and the streets were jammed with people, some of whom called out in recognition to him. But Leka would not stop for anyone. He just kept going, even though each step was an agony, and his mouth and throat were parched with thirst.

Leka's strength had just about given out by the time he reached the marina, but when he saw the *Crazy Horse*, he let out a loud bark. Immediately Ben jumped up from the galley. Seconds later the two of them were reunited on the dock, with Ben crying out, "Leka, Leka, Leka!" and hugging and nuzzling the dog. Leka was equally excited and forgot all his aches and pains as he barked and licked Ben's face, his tail snapping around wildly, deliriously.

Chapter Twelve

With Zoe's help, Ben healed Leka's wounds and got him cleaned up and looking like his old self again. When the dog seemed healthy and strong, Ben made plans to leave Kos for Athens. Ben was unhappy to be parted from Zoe and Nikos, if only for a few weeks, but he was eager to put Kos behind him. The kidnapper, whoever he was, was still around, which made remaining here too risky. It was only when he had pulled up anchor and put out to sea that Ben felt safe again.

As they sailed westward through the heart of the Aegean, going from one Greek island to another, Ben's spirits began to lift. His desire to draw returned, and he began to work with a pen or pencil every day, making sketches of each island they visited. As for Leka, he too felt better and began to put back on the weight and luster he had lost. He also became a more patient model for Ben. Normally, he was unable to stay in one place very long, but now he seemed less restless, and Ben didn't have to keep begging, "Sit, Leka, sit," while sketching him. It was as if the dog understood, the way Ben did, how easily their relationship could be shattered by forces beyond their control, forces as sudden and wayward as a kidnapper's evil act.

Their time together became more precious, if only because they had learned that happiness was like one of those groupers Ben speared in the sea. One minute it was in your hand, the next it twisted away and disappeared.

Ben's luck at fishing also came back. He began to bring in big fish again, at least one a week, and lots of smaller ones as well—bream, mullet and perch. He also took numerous lobster, wild oysters and other shellfish.

Every day became an adventure, both where the diving and the sailing were concerned. The closer they got to the Cyclades, the circle of islands forming the center of the Aegean, the harder the winds blew.

Ben tried hard to maintain his northerly position so that he wasn't always sailing directly into the teeth of the meltemi, but in the end the force of the wind defeated him and pushed him off course. Ultimately, he quit trying to battle the meltemi and simply altered his schedule, sailing only in the hours before and after sunrise, when the wind was manageable. As soon as it kicked up, he took shelter somewhere and sat things out until the next day.

The Cyclades Islands were different from

the islands of the Dodecanese, more barren and rocky. The houses were smaller and more compact, without any interior courtyards and gardens, but they were beautiful in their own right, scattered like sugar cubes over the flanks of brown hills topped with windmills and chapels that gleamed whitely in the hard light of the sun.

To sail the Cyclades was to penetrate to the heart of Greece. At the dead center was the island of Delos. It was a small island, but at one time it had been an important place, a sacred island. Today, Delos was a tourist attraction. People came daily from other islands to visit the archaeological sites. Remnants of an ancient city were on display—the Sun God Apollo's Sanctuary, the House of Cleopatra, the crumbling ruins of a theater quarter. There were temples, baths and athletic fields, columns that had once supported elaborate statuary.

Because there was only one small hotel on Delos, most tourists left the island by nightfall, and it reverted back to its silent, deserted character.

Ben didn't mind the silence that permeated the night air. He had dropped anchor in the main port and, when the *Crazy Horse* was tied up securely, gone ashore with Leka to look around. There was a full moon which shed such a strong light that he didn't need a flashlight. Although the museums were closed, it was still possible to wander around the streets that formed the western border of the ancient city.

87

Lying in the dust were fragments of sculptures and shards of clay pots and lamps that had once been used by the island's inhabitants.

Ben made his way to the famed Delian Lions,a gift of the people of the island of Naxos. Of the nine stone lions that had once occupied the terrace, only five remained, but they looked amazingly well-preserved and imposing. Even Leka seemed impressed with them, and stood staring fixedly at them in the moonlight for the longest time.

When they returned to the *Crazy Horse*, Leka curled up on his coil of rope and went to sleep, but Ben sat up on deck with his back to the mast, looking across at Delos and letting his mind spool out. Again, he thought of his parents, who would have enjoyed visiting such a famous place as this. With their interest in history and archaeology, they probably would have wanted to anchor here for a week or so, giving them time to explore the entire island.

But Ben did not have that kind of time to spare. He had to push extra hard to get to Athens to meet the Smiths. Without an engine to power the *Crazy Horse*, he had to depend on the winds to carry him along. Trouble was, the meltemi was fickle thing, howling like a hyena for days at a time, only to suddenly turn mysteriously silent and still.

Ben had heard stories of sailboats becoming becalmed in the Cyclades and drifting along under a listless canvas while the Greek sun beat down on them, reflecting off the smooth, shiny surface of the sea with pitiless intensity. Ben could not afford to lose this charter. While the money he had made from his sketches and paintings was enough to keep him alive, he needed to be able to put something aside to tide him over the winter months.

It was too dangerous to sail the Aegean in winter, when severe storms from the south blew up at regular intervals. He would have to find a safe harbor in which to sit out the bad months. That meant no charters and no tourists around to buy his sketches. There wouldn't be much spearfishing either, not when the storms churned up the sea and made visibility difficult.

With all this in mind, Ben hauled up anchor and set sail for Athens again. No waiting out the worst of the meltemi either—he had to push on through the Cyclades, as fast as he could.

The meltemi kept blowing, fighting him every minute of the day and night. What a tough, capricious wind it was, sometimes blowing straight and hard, other times swirling round and round, making it necessary for him to keep changing the sails as he tacked this way and that. Because he was alone, Ben had to do all the work himself. Soon his hands were rubbed raw, and his back became sore and stiff. But he couldn't quit, not if he were to reach Athens on schedule.

This kind of voyage was a good test of a sailor's mettle. Ben learned a lot about himself—how long he could go without rest, how much discomfort and pain he could stand. The wind lashed at him like a salty whip and made his eyes burn and tear. The sun scorched his skin and turned it dark and hard. The sea pounded away at the *Crazy Horse*, socking it with strong, choppy waves that made the cat shake and shudder. But still Ben pushed on, one eye on the compass, another on the sails, steering the *Crazy Horse* with all the skill he could muster.

Something else was driving him now, something he didn't quite understand. It had nothing to do with money or seamanship. It went much deeper than that, a powerful emotion he had never felt before. All he knew was that he was gripped by it and had to obey it, even if it meant disregarding Lukas' advice about the importance of respecting and fearing Mother Nature. Try as he might, he could not be cautious now, could not hold back from taking on the meltemi, defying it, pushing on through it. Leka stayed by his side the whole time, gamely riding out the wind—the infamous meltemi which never seemed to flag. It was was a wind from hell, and it was making this voyage a torture, but Ben refused to give in to it, refused to find shelter. He just soldiered on, a defiant, mad kind of look in his eyes.

Of the two of them, Leka had much better control of his emotions right now. His courage and confidence ran so deep that Ben was put to shame. Leka had become grown up and brave, he realized. Not that Leka didn't still like to make merry on shore—his carefree, fun-loving spirit would never desert him. But here at sea, with the two of them battling the elements like this, Leka understood that he needed to be calm and poised, if only to reassure his wild-eyed young master. In a way, their positions had become reversed. When Ben first met Leka, he had done the caring and nurturing. But now that Leka had matured, it was he who was doing the looking after.

Ben felt cheered every time he glanced at Leka, because no matter how much the wind howled and the catamaran heeled and shook and shuddered, the dog never whined, never showed fear. He sat with upright head and cocked ears, looking into the teeth of the meltemi with supreme confidence. Ben took strength from that and began to feel less anxious and driven himself.

It was as if Leka had become the master and Ben the pup.

The closest Cycladic island to Athens was Kea. A craggy, mountainous place, it had a rugged beauty that pleased Ben. From the sea it had looked gray and rocky, but once he and Leka went ashore, they discovered hidden, fertile valleys and prosperous villages.

Because of its proximity to Athens—two hours by ferryboat—many yacht owners from the mainland kept their vessels here, either in St. Nicholas Bay, one of the safest, all-weather moorings in the Aegean, or in the town of Vourkari, which was built around a deep inlet and had numerous shops and restaurants.

It was always pleasant to walk along the harbor of a Greek island at dusk. Yachts riding

91

at anchor were a colorful sight with their brightly-colored sails and white-painted hulls contrasting with the dark blue of the Aegean. There was much hustle and bustle—men hawking lottery tickets or fresh fish or pungent-smelling natural sponges; families out for a stroll; waiters beckoning from the doorways of coffee houses and tavernas. Music was in the air, gulls circled overhead cawing for food, children ran and laughed at play. It was a warm, homey scene, and Ben felt his heart gladden with every step.

Best of all was to suddenly encounter a familiar face—that of his friend and mentor, Dick Matson. Dick's little sailboat *Old Glory* was moored off the furthest end of the quay, some distance from the other boats. Dick had picked this spot because he was making repairs on his boat, which hadn't fared well in the recent meltemi.

"I scraped against an unmarked reef while trying to find shelter off the island of Syros," he told Ben. "It damaged the keel and opened a few seams. I've been sitting here for a week patching *Old Glory* up. Once she's seaworthy again, I'll head to a boatyard in Athens and haul her out of the water for more extensive repairs."

The potential cost of all this work had Dick worried. "What I earn with my paintings and fishing will never cover my bills. I think I'm going to have to take a job in Athens and work all winter long to raise some extra money," he confided.

"What will you do? The Greek government doesn't give foreigners work permits that easily," Ben said.

"True, but one can always teach English privately. It's hard work, but it pays well."

Ben wasn't used to seeing the usually cheerful and boyish-looking Dick show such a glum, downcast face. In order to take Dick's mind off his problems, Ben suggested that they go out diving together.

They borrowed a rubber boat from one of Dick's friends and chugged out to a small, uninhabited island off Kea. They found a cove and allowed Leka to jump ashore and explore to his heart's content while they donned their wetsuits, loaded their spearguns and started hunting in depths of the sea.

Soon Dick spotted a grouper and went down and chased it under a rock. But the fish escaped down a deep shaft and could not be found. Cursing their bad luck, they resumed the hunt.

Conditions were favorable. The sea was calm and visibility was good, though a strong current was running along the bottom. A little while later Ben spotted another grouper. Water magnifies, especially at the fish's depth, but Ben estimated it to be between twenty-five and thirty-five pounds—the biggest fish he had ever encountered while diving in Greece.

The grouper was smart and slid under a boulder, but not hastily, a good sign. It meant he wasn't spooked. Ben swam round to the far side of the boulder and started his dive from

93

there, so that the fish couldn't see him coming. It was a long, slow dive and so deep that
his mask squeezed hard against his face, hurting his nose. But the current wasn't as bad as
he feared, and his wind was good by the time
he reached the boulder and crept round it, body
brushing along the bottom, gun and flashlight
at the ready.

The fish was lying in the left corner of the
crevice, his big, thick head pointed down-
wards. Ben had time to shine his light on him,
line up a shot, and fire.

There was an immediate commotion as the
spear hit, and the fish reacted, making the
spear vibrate wildly, like a diving rod. But the
grouper was so thick and strong the spear
hardly penetrated.

Time to go up for air and let Dick dive and
put a second shot in the fish—a killing shot,
hopefully. Lungs heaving, head throbbing, Ben
lay on the surface, watching as Dick descend-
ed, carving a graceful semi-circle as he headed toward the boulder, flippered feet kicking
rhythmically, one hand pinching his nose to
clear the pressure on his ears.

When Dick reached the bottom, he pulled
aside the line holding Ben's gun, the better to
get a look at things. From the way Dick was
pointing his flashlight, Ben knew that the
grouper had retreated into the far corner of
the crevice and that his head was hidden from
view, which meant Dick was unable to kill him
with his second shot.

Once he had surfaced and got his breath

back, Dick confirmed the position of the fish, adding that he didn't think they could extricate him from that particular spot.

"He's opened his gills and spines like a man bracing himself in a doorway," he said. "But there is a back door to the boulder. I could see it clearly, and it's a big one. We should be able to pull him out from there."

It called for more teamwork. Someone had to dive around to the far side and shoot the fish again, with a third gun. The next man had to dive on the original side and cut the lines holding the first two spears. Then and only then could an attempt be made to pull the grouper out of the rear side of the rock.

Ben swam back to his float and untied his spare gun, a big, three-band Arbalete. He had bought it second-hand in a shop on Kos, only to discover it had a skittish firing mechanism, one that sometimes released the spear without the trigger being pulled. Now was the time to use it, though.

Trouble was, it would take another ten feet of diving to reach the far side of the boulder, enter the opening and propel himself upward to be able to get close enough to fire with any accuracy. Ben lay on the surface, breathing slowly and deeply for some minutes. Then he loaded the Arbalete carefully, with the safety on. Then, pointing the gun away from him, he released the safety, fully expecting the trigger to fire on its own.

Surprise. The grip held. Ben swam toward the open sea, passing Dick, placing himself so that he would have the current behind him when he dove. He felt a keen, tingling sense of excitement. This was what spearfishing was all about—not the killing of fish, but the diving, the challenge. At the same time, he felt a touch of apprehension as well. He was about to dive deeper than he had ever dived before—a good fifty-five or sixty feet.

Gulping down as much air as he could, Ben started down, adjusting his ears every ten feet or so as the pressure kept squeezing against him—not just his ears but his body. His heart pounded away in his chest.

Then he reached the boulder and crept under it, telling himself to stay calm and make the shot good. He didn't need a flashlight to see the fish. It lay with its head turned toward him, framed by the band of sunlight penetrating the crevice. Ben inched as close as he dared, aimed and fired. The grouper went still.

No more wind. Backing out of the boulder, Ben turned and looked up. Through the shafts of sunlight streaming down into the depths he could see Dick lying spread-eagled on the surface, staring wide-eyed at him through his mask.

Up and up, Ben went, feeling tired but good. As he broke the surface and gulped air down into his lungs, he signaled for Dick to make his dive. Dick's mission was to cut the lines of the first two spears, which he did, in a matter of seconds.

When Ben was rested he made another dive, ducking under the boulder from the far side again. He wriggled upwards, reached in for the spear and pulled on it. The fish didn't budge. With his breath beginning to run out, Ben yanked again, with both hands. This time the fish slid a few inches closer. Ben reached for the fish's head, grabbed hard and pulled again. With the last strength in him, Ben gave another heave and pulled the fish out of its lair.

Ben started up, holding the grouper tightly. The extra weight made the ascent long, slow and difficult. He had to pump with all his might to reach the surface, but once he did, Dick was there to help, taking the fish from him and heading to shore with it while Ben lay sucking down air into his lungs and tasting the rich, sweet wine of victory.

Chapter Thirteen

They celebrated later by joining a Greek family that had invited them to a panayiri—a celebration in honor of one of the island's patron saints. It was to be held at a small hilltop chapel about five miles away from Vourkari. Because the only road that led to the chapel was narrow and unpaved, they would have to ride donkeys to get there. Leka, of course, had to walk up the hill.

It was Ben and Dick's first time on a donkey. They kept laughing as they rode up the mountain on the backs of these small, sturdy creatures, their long legs almost brushing against the ground. And every time one of the donkeys brayed they laughed even harder. After a while, though, they began to grow fond of these squat beasts of burden. They may have looked and sounded funny, but they never faltered or slipped, no matter how heavy the load or steep the trail. Leka kept glancing up at Ben as they trotted along, not quite believing what he saw. Ben held tight to the reins as they climbed. The saddle under him was a simple thing, leather braced with wood but not uncomfortable. Around the donkey's head was a leather harness decorated with blue beads meant to ward off the evil eye. Ben made a mental note to attach similar blue beads to Leka's collar.

They passed terraced places of hard-earned greenery. Olives, grapes, almonds and oaks grew in fields that were separated from each other by stone walls. Some of the farmers kept sheep, goats and cows as well. Hawks circled in the sky overhead and crickets raised a clatter in the trees and shrubs. The sunlight poured down relentlessly, scorching the earth and everything that moved on it.

Ben and Dick's hosts were the Simonides family, descendants of a famous local scribe in classical times who went to Athens and became the equivalent of a poet laureate, writing elegies, epigrams and dirges on demand for the royal family.

Pavlos Simonides, who was Ben's age, met them at the top of the mountain. Pavlos was black-haired, cheerful and hardy. He led everyone across to a nearby field where an ancient statue stood, the figure of another lion. Carved out of a single block of green rock by an unknown sculptor around 600 BC, it reminded Ben of the lions he had seen on Delos, with a distinctive difference—this one had a smile on its face!

It came as a jolt to see it. Normally lions were represented as stern, magisterial and forbidding, but this creature wore a smile as big and curved as a slice of watermelon. To study it was to bring a smile to your own face, which was probably what the artist had intended.

Even Leka was drawn to the sly, humorous look on the lion's face. After staring at it, he looked over at Ben, who was, of course, grinning from ear to ear. Leka's tail began to snap around excitedly, and he seemed to smile himself.

Hundreds of islanders greeted them when they reached their final destination, a small hilltop monastery. Black-garbed women swarmed all over the site, some cleaning up the chapel and the grounds around it, others unpacking baskets of food and wine. The air smelled of baking bread and fresh-cut flowers and herbs.

Kea's main religious festival had been celebrated in mid-August, but, as Pavlos explained, there were many minor celebrations as well. With some four hundred churches for the eighteen hundred inhabitants of Kea, there was probably a festive occasion happening just about every day of the year.

Today's ceremony commenced when the priest arrived, also on the back of a donkey. The priest had a suitcase in hand and soon changed into his formal robes. Soon he was saying prayers in the chapel and swinging an incense-burner around. Pavlos and his family led the chanting and singing, with others joining in from time to time, their voices rising high and floating over the hilltop. By now dusk had settled on the scene. Candles and lanterns provided the only illumination. When the religious ceremony was concluded, the Simonides family began passing out chunks of fresh bread to everyone gathered there. Five musicians unpacked their instruments and began to tune up. They sat under a plane tree, lit by the bluish glare of a pump-up lantern, large glasses of wine and ouzo by their sides.

In a nearby grove of trees was tethered a small flock of goats and sheep. Leka crossed to have a look at the animals. Ben did not go with him, because he and Dick had been pulled on to the dance floor—just a level patch of dirt—and urged to take part in a susta by the Simondes family.

The susta was a folk dance. Half a dozen people linked arms and danced in slow, rhythmic fashion while the leader capered about freely, gaily. It was a dance that combined the steadiness and discipline of Greek island people with their more spontaneous, volatile side. It was also a dance that went back thousands of years, connecting these modern folk to their ancestors. They danced in praise of the saints, the goodness of God, the bountifulness of life.

Ben got so caught up in the revels that he failed to hear Leka's sudden, angry yelp. He had no idea what was happening over there in the darkness. A wolf had crept down from his mountain lair, attracted by the scent given off by the goats and sheep. He hid behind a shrub, a lean, gray, hard-eyed creature with a big hunger. He had lived in these hills all his life,

101

preying on smaller, weaker game for sustenance.

Most of the tethered goats and sheep were kids, prized for their tender, succulent meat. They were also weak, fearful creatures—easy pickings for the wolf. But Leka wasn't about to let the wolf attack the flock—his instinct as a guard dog would not allow such a thing to happen, not without a battle.

As for the wolf, he wasn't used to facing a dog like Leka. The few dogs he had encountered over the years were afraid of him, especially when he bared his fangs and glared at them, growling low and menacingly in his throat. They had always backed off, even run away, when he advanced.

Not Leka, though. He stood his ground, legs spread wide apart, ears cocked back, body tensed and ready, eyes fixed alertly on the wolf. He began to make menacing noises of his own, a growl that came from his powerful chest.

Leka took a step toward the wolf, giving a loud, aggressive bark. Startled, the wolf backed up a few paces, but he kept growling, threatening to attack. Leka kept advancing on him, sounding a last warning. The wolf refused to heed it.

Leka leapt at his adversary, going for his throat. The wolf, giving a cry of fear, tried to twist away. When Leka's teeth sank into his flesh, his immediate response was to fight back. The wolf was strong and cunning, but he was no match for Leka, who had become a different dog now, a tough, ferocious battler.

One more bite was all it took for the wolf to lose courage. Wrenching out of Leka's grasp, he gave a howl of pain and took off for the darkness and safety of the forest.

Leka, breathing heavily, body trembling with suppressed violence, stood watching the wolf go. He could have pursued him, but chose not to. He had fought to save the goats and sheep, not to kill. His job was done.

Later, after he had calmed down, Leka returned to the festival. The dancing was still going on, as it would all night. Ben excused himself and crossed to check Leka out. "You all right?" he asked, studying the dog intently.

Leka made a soft noise in his throat and rubbed his body against Ben's leg in friendly, reassuring fashion, as if nothing at all had happened to him.

Chapter Fourteen

The port town of Athens is called Piraeus. It was founded in the fifth century BC by a king named Themistocles. Today it was an overcrowded, noisy and bustling metropolis divided into various districts. The marina for private boats was called Tourkolimani, and that's where Ben headed in the *Crazy Horse*, dropping anchor and sending Leka ashore with the line. Once the cat was moored, Ben set off on foot to find the office of his charter agency, with Leka following behind. They climbed up a steep hill from the harbor and followed a curving waterfront road for nearly a mile. It was a bright, clear day, and Ben was feeling in high spirits. They had crossed almost the entire length of the Aegean and arrived safely.

His happiness evaporated, though, when he reached the agency and was handed a telex from the Smiths. "A serious illness in the family obliges us to cancel our charter trip with you," the message read. "Sorry for this, but it is simply impossible for us to leave Paris at this time. We hope we can make the trip with you next year."

That was it. There was no mention of paying him even a part of the money coming to him.

The message was a week old. "We tried to relay it to you," the agent said, "but as you don't have a ship-to-shore radio aboard your boat, we had no way of finding you. Next time, check with us each time you reach a new port."

Next time.

Next time, I will do things differently, Ben told himself as he trooped back to Tourkolimani. Next time I will get a hefty deposit when I book a charter. Next time I will not be so naïve and trusting as to take people at their word. Next time I will not have anything to do with people like the Smiths.

In the days that followed, Ben made the rounds of the other yacht agencies in the area, trying to find a replacement charter. But it was late in the year, and bookings were hard to come by, though Ben did find a family looking for a one-week charter around the nearby Saronic Gulf. But the mother was allergic to dogs, and the father refused to sail on a boat that wasn't equipped with an auxiliary engine.

So Ben stayed put in Tourkolimani, waiting for Zoe and Nikos to arrive from Kos. He passed his time by doing more sketches of Leka. The waters around Piraeus and Athens were dirty and polluted, so spearfishing was out of the question. At night he went to one of

105

the numerous outdoor cinemas in Piraeus. It was pleasant to sit under the stars in the warm weather and watch an old American movie with Greek sub-titles. Halfway through the feature there was a fifteen-minute break during which small children came round peddling cold drinks and ice cream. Because the Greeks did not believe in babysitters, whole families could be found here at night, including screaming infants.

Both Ben and Leka were cheered when Zoe, Nikos, and Hector finally showed up, after having put Mark on a plane to London. School was starting next week for Nikos, and he wasn't looking forward to it. "The teachers and kids are okay," he told Ben, "but it's located in the hills above Athens and is a long way from the sea. No more diving for me, not until next summer."

Nikos had brought with him his mask, snorkel and flippers. "I'm going to have a look around the harbor," he said. "There's all kinds of good stuff on the bottom, things the boat people have dropped overboard. Why don't you come out with me? Maybe you'll be lucky enough to find a Rolex."

Ben begged off, explaining that Zoe had invited him to lunch.

"Okay, then. Yassou," Nikos said, heading toward the far end of the dock, dive bag in hand, Hector and Leka following.

Ben and Zoe found a waterfront table. It was protected by a mushroom-like sun umbrella. From here they could look out over the harbor

106

while they ate. Zoe ordered grilled lobster and a bottle of cold retsina. She looked fresh and summery in her white shift and straw hat decorated with plastic flowers. They chatted as they ate and drank. She reported that the first results of the mail-order campaign on his book were promising. The replies were coming in, accompanied with checks. "I think we're going to do well with the book," she said. "People love your sketches of Leka."

Pleased, Ben sipped his wine and nibbled on his lobster. He caught sight of Nikos swimming around in the water, looking for sunglasses and jewelry. Ben also noticed the captain of a nearby sailboat struggling to raise his anchor.

It happened all the time in crowded harbors like Tourkolimani. With so many boats packed shoulder to shoulder, it was inevitable that lines should become entangled and snarled. Usually it was possible to free your anchor by much winching and hauling, but this particular skipper was not having any luck. The more he struggled and used his engine to go backward and forward, the worse it got for him. After a half hour of it, he gave up the battle and looked for a diver to help.

In this case the diver was Nikos. Though Ben couldn't hear what was being said out there, he knew the skipper was offering the boy money to free his anchor. The water was not too deep, no more than twenty feet, so Nikos would not have any problems on that score.

It was hard work to free an anchor, though. It took numerous dives and much expenditure of energy. Nikos went up and down again and again, pausing only long enough to clear his snorkel, gulp down some air, and head for the bottom once more. Ben watched him for a while, then he turned back to Zoe and his lunch.

A little while later he was aware of Leka's bark. It wasn't his ordinary bark, a happy little yelp. This was his agitated bark—his panicked bark—and it was directed at him!

Ben immediately divined what had happened. Grabbing a sharp knife from the table, he flew as fast as he could toward the dock. Leka, waiting for him there, dove in the water and headed out into the middle of the harbor. Ben threw himself into the sea with all his clothes on and followed Leka as swiftly as he could.

Leka stopped and dog-paddled, still barking furiously, marking the spot where Nikos had last been seen. Ben dove down and kicked with all his might to reach the bottom. The water was murky, stained with gas and oil. Ben's eyes burned, but he managed to keep them open as he looked this way and that for a sign of Nikos. The harbor floor was covered not just with anchors, but also with all kinds of junk—boxes, plastic containers, wine and soda bottles. Anchor lines crisscrossed every which way, making a kind of underwater spider's web. In the middle of it, thrashing around in desperation, was Nikos.

With his lungs beginning to ache from the exertion, Ben swam as fast as he could to reach the boy. He could see that Nikos, in trying to free the boat's anchor line, had lifted one of the anchor's prongs, only to get snarled in the line when the heavy anchor suddenly shifted position.

Nikos pulled this way and that on the line but could not free himself. He began to panic and struggle frantically. This final, desperate expenditure of energy cost him—the snorkel came out of his mouth, and his head rolled back as he passed out.

Ben grabbed the line and began to saw away at it with his knife. The line wasn't all that thick, but the pressure of the water made his work difficult and slow. His own breath began to give out, and his eyes began to blur. Summoning up all his strength and resolve, Ben made a last, desperate attempt to cut Nikos free.

Finally the line parted, releasing its tension. Slipping an arm around Nikos' chest, Ben put his feet on the soft, mushy bottom and shoved himself upwards, kicking hard. It was the most difficult thing he had ever done, carrying Nikos to the surface, but he managed it.

A quick-witted sailor had rowed his dinghy out to where Leka, still treading water and barking furiously, was marking the spot. When Ben broke water, the sailor grabbed hold of Nikos and hauled him up into the boat, immediately beginning to give him mouth-to-mouth resuscitation.

For a few long seconds Nikos did not respond. But then his body gave a shudder, his lungs began to work, and his eyes fluttered open. Overjoyed, Ben threw his arms around the young boy and hugged him with all his might.

Chapter Fifteen

Nikos' blackout in the sea could have caused serious damage, not to speak of death, had it lasted just a few more seconds, said the doctor who tended him in the Piraeus hospital.

"It was that close," he told Ben and Zoe. "You're lucky that Leka sounded an immediate warning—and that you were able to follow through on the rescue."

When Nikos was fully recovered, Zoe held off putting him in school. By way of celebration, she, Nikos, Hector, Leka and Ben took a trip in the *Crazy Horse* to the nearby island of Aegina, dropping anchor at Agia Marina. The next day Ben and Zoe rented a car and set off to see the island, especially the ruins of the fifth-century Temple of Aphaea. Nikos preferred to remain in Agia Marina and have fun with Hector and Leka.

The site of the Temple and the adjoining Hellenic ruins were located on a hillside covered with cactus and briars, but it offered a panoramic view of the island, most of which was covered with olive, fig and pistachio groves. It was a warm September day with sunlight glistening on the blue Aegean and crickets making a racket in the trees.

Ben and Zoe shared a picnic lunch, finishing it off with a handful of fat, ripe figs that Ben had picked for them. After a little rest they resumed their swing around the island, which turned out to be filled with modern villages, high mountains and rocky coves. It was late in the afternoon by the time they returned to the marina. Ben whistled for Leka, waiting for him to come running up to greet him. Instead it was Nikos who came racing toward them, his face contorted with anguish and fear.

"Something's the matter with the dogs!" he shouted.

"Where are they?"

Nikos pointed to the dock. Zoe gave a scream when she saw Hector lying there on his side stiffly, not moving. As for Leka, Ben spotted him swimming in circles just off the starboard side of the *Crazy Horse*.

Zoe knelt down by Hector's side, checking him out.

"What happened?" Ben asked the distraught Nikos. "Were they in a fight? Did other dogs attack them?"

The boy shook his head vigorously. "We were together all day, except for a few minutes here and there when they chased a cat or something. The dogs seemed fine until we came back here, and then Hector suddenly started having some kind of fit, Leka, too. Hector collapsed and Leka jumped into the sea."

"Did they eat any strange food?" Zoe asked.

"Well, when we went through the market they picked up a few scraps of meat."

"The meat was poisoned!" Zoe cried out, pointing to the green foam caking Hector's lips.

"Oh, my God," Nikos said, in tears. "I never thought anything was wrong. Butchers on Kos were always giving them bits of something to eat."

"That was our island. Here not everyone is a friend."

Ben checked Hector's heartbeat. Nothing. He glanced at Leka, who was swimming round and round in tight little circles, a look of terror and agony in his eyes.

Ben threw himself into the sea and swam out to Leka as fast as he could. He grabbed him and held on to his cold, shivering body as he returned to the pier. A couple of passersby helped haul them out of the water.

Leka went into convulsions that were so violent Ben knew the end was near. "What should I do?" he asked Zoe.

"The only hope is to give him an emetic, something to clean him out!"

Ben jumped aboard the *Crazy Horse* and raced down below for the bottle of olive oil, the gift from Lukas. It had saved Leka's life once; maybe it would save it again.

Ben returned to Leka's side and took hold of him. With Zoe's help, he forced Leka's mouth open and poured the olive oil down his throat, half the bottle.

Leka made a retching noise— the contents of his stomach came out, and soon the convulsions began to ease up. Leka no longer fought for breath so desperately. Ben poured the rest of the bottle down Hector's gullet, but to no avail. It was too late, nothing could be done for him.

He turned back to Leka. The same green foam oozed out of Leka's throat and formed on his mouth. A few moments later, he coughed up more horrible-looking stuff and lay breathing heavily. Finally, he managed to get to his feet and stand there shakily, sucking air down into his lungs as he gazed with doleful eyes at Hector.

In the days that followed, Ben stayed by Zoe's side as she paced the streets of Agia Marina in her grief. Sometimes Nikos and Leka joined them, though the latter was still weak and could not walk far. Nikos tried to take the blame for what had happened, but Ben and Zoe wouldn't let him. It wasn't his fault that the dogs had been the inadvertent targets of a police campaign aimed at holding down the street animal population.

When Ben and Zoe went to the station to lodge an official complaint, the chief expressed his regrets over the occurrence. "We were instructed to do something about the large number of stray dogs and cats in the port. We did not mean to harm anyone's pets. But it's not our fault you allowed your dogs to run around without a leash," he added.

"We would have kept the dogs on the boat, if we had known you were going to put poison out," Zoe said to him. "Why didn't you make an announcement?"

"It didn't seem necessary. So few Greeks keep pets," he explained. "They tend to abandon them after the summer holidays or when they move. Some of the animals become wild and dangerous. We have to protect ourselves from them as best we can."

"Provisions could have been made for these animals to be rounded up and put in kennels."

The chief just shrugged his shoulders. "I'm just following orders," he explained. "The instructions came from the public health office. Complain to them if you want."

Ben and Zoe did just that, but got nowhere. In Greece the traditional way to get rid of stray animals was to poison them. It was a simple and quick solution to a complex problem.

"There are better and more humane ways to hold down the number of unwanted cats and dogs than by killing them," Zoe insisted. "Why don't you neuter or sterilize the animals? That's what they do in most other countries."

"It's a good idea," the official allowed, "but we don't do it that way."

"Can't you change your ways?"

"I don't make policy," came the reply. "I simply do what I'm told."

Zoe's response to such callousness was to fight back by forming a foundation which would educate Greek people about the rights of animals. The foundation would also lobby for a law forbidding the use of poison as a means of eliminating unwanted cats and dogs.

It would encourage the authorities—and pet owners as well—to employ spaying and sterilization instead. The foundation would push for a series of animal shelters to be built in Greece: large, clean facilities containing boarding kennels, hospitals and clinics, with office space for full-time veterinarians and staff.

It was an ambitious program, one that wouldn't be easy to put across in a country where change came slowly. But Zoe knew that most Greeks were decent, kind people and would respond in a positive fashion to the foundation's efforts. It was a question of changing inherited ways of thinking about street animals. This could only be brought about with a strong promotional campaign, especially in the schools.

"That's where you and Leka could help," Zoe said to Ben. "You could visit schools and talk about animal rights. The kids would then teach their parents in turn."

Ben thought about it. He was tempted to stay in Tourkolimani for the winter, living on the boat with Leka, helping Zoe with her foundation, seeing Nikos on weekends. He could also help Dick Matson repair *Old Glory* once the sailboat had been hauled out of the water and put up on blocks.

All that sounded pretty good. Leka would be especially happy to visit schools and make friends with children. But when Ben sat by himself in the cockpit of the *Crazy Horse* that evening, sipping a cold drink, enjoying a spectacular red-sky sunset, he came to the conclusion that he had to move on.

It was too soon to give up sailing and diving, even for a few months. The *Crazy Horse* was a new boat and didn't need to be taken out of action, the way *Old Glory* did. The cat should keep sailing, long and hard. Ben felt sure of it. The thing that had made him drive on so recklessly through the meltemi was now clear to him.

His parents had given up a safe, comfortable life as school teachers to become full-time sailors. Ben was very much their child, a child of the sea, as it were. It was his destiny to be a captain, to keep on adventuring in the *Crazy Horse*.

That's all they had wanted out of life, to be skippers of their own vessel, sailing far, sailing wide, sailing free. Death had robbed them of that dream, but now Ben was living it for them. That's why he had to keep going, keep voyaging.

The next morning he told Zoe and Nikos of his plans. He would leave Tourkolimani in a few days and head north, to the island of Malta. From there he would sail to Sardinia, Italy and then to Ibiza, Spain, finishing his two-month trip in Gibraltar, where, if his book of sketches sold as Zoe thought it might, he would spend the profits on the *Crazy Horse*, putting in an engine and other important equipment.

Then he would find someone to help train

Leka with his toilet habits. Once that was done, he and Leka would take on the challenge of sailing across the Atlantic. It would be just the two of them, facing months and months at sea—a vast, endless, perilous sea. They would be the first man and dog to make such a crossing, and if they survived it, they would continue on to the Caribbean, braving the very body of water that had claimed his parents' lives.

Ben owed it to them to complete the journey they had started but were unable to finish. Then, and only then, could he feel at peace with himself.

Ben and Leka's Journey

GLOSSARY

Becalmed	To be rendered motionless due to lack of wind
Bollard	A strong post, securing lines
Bouboulitsa	A common small Aegean fish, usually black
Bouzouki	A long, stringed instrument that resembles a mandolin
Bow	The forward point of a boat
Caiques	Aegean boats that can hold goods and products
Caravida	Lobster found in the Aegean
Force Seven	Near gale force winds
Halyards	Lines used to haul up the sail
Keel	The main structural member of a boat's hull, running bow to stern
Leecloth	A shelter or cover to keep dry or secure
Loukoumia	A soft jelly candy with powdered sugar topping

Mainsail	Sail set on the mainmast
Mainsheet	Line securing the mainsail
Meltemi	The famous Greek wind that sweeps across the Aegean
On the beam	Going across the width of a boat, either wind or waves
Port	The left-hand side of a boat
Quay	A wharf, a protected harbor
Retsina	A unique Greek wine
Shrouds	Lines from the mast top
Sheets	Ropes used to set the sail
Starboard	The right-hand side of a boat
Staysail	Triangular, smaller sail attached to stays
Taverna	Small restuarant
To flag	To become feeble
Tiller	Lever used to turn a boat's rudder to change course

About the Author

Willard Manus was born and raised in New York City but lived for many years in the Greek islands, mostly in the village of Lindos, on the island of Rhodes. His experiences there were published in a memoir, *This Way to Paradise—Dancing on the Tables*. While living in the Aegean, he also wrote novels, plays and articles—and learned how to sail and spearfish.

Printed in the United States
83838LV00002B/166-189/A

9 780974 055138